# *The*
# PEARL
## *of great price*

*a novel by*
# PAUL E. TSIKA

# The Pearl
## of Great Price

A Novel by

Paul E. Tsika

Plow On Publications

Midfield, TX

Scriptures are taken from the New King James Version, English Standard Version, and The Message.

ISBN 978-0-9851797-2-4


Plow On Publications
a Division of Paul E. Tsika Ministries, Inc.
Restoration Ranch
P. O. Box 136
Midfield, TX  77458
www.plowon.org


Printed in the United States of America

# Dedication

When I think of how my life has been impacted for Christ there are several names that come to mind. These men have been my mentors in the Faith.

Manley Beasley who taught me the "ways" of God.
Ron Dunn who taught me the "word" of God.
Jack Taylor who taught me the "worship" of God.

Manley and Ron passed from this life years ago and are enjoying the fruits of their labors for Christ's Kingdom. Jack is still traveling, more anointed than ever, and being greatly used of the Lord to make a difference in Christ's Kingdom here on earth.

But this book, however, is a special dedication to my former pastor at Milldale Baptist Church in Zachary, Louisiana, Bro. Jimmy Robertson, who taught me of the "work" of God. He demonstrated to me, daily, what it means to labor in God's vineyard. Bro. Jimmy and his godly wife, Frances, have three wonderful children and have been blessed with grandchildren and great grandchildren.

Bro. Jimmy founded Milldale Baptist Church, Milldale Bible Conference, Fires of Revival Paper and Milldale International Ministries. These ministries alone have been responsible for distributing over one billion (with a "B") pieces of Christian literature around the world. Bibles, tracts, books and other literature were  sent free of charge for multiplied years.

Milldale Baptist Church has been the foundation for many outreaches to bless the Christian community, through Milldale Bible Conference and Fires of Revival Paper.  Thousands have been saved, made right with God, surrendered to preach, and sent to the mission field under his ministry.

Some of the most anointed and noted men and women of God of the last two generations have spoken at Milldale's conferences.  Tens of thousands have been fed and housed on the ground all because a young man from Tickfaw, Louisiana, was visited by the Holy Ghost in an old dairy barn.

Often times Bro. Jimmy would find himself shut up to God for a time of prayer and fasting…in a hunting camp for days… near the swamps… with only a jug of water.  He would emerge with a word from God and direction for the church and camp.

When Bro. Jimmy preached on missions you wanted to sell everything you had and lay it on the altar. Time and time again we would end up shaking our heads over God's provision. Monies would come from totally unexpected sources to buy paper to print Bibles or make needed repairs on the camp grounds. We witnessed God's power and longed for more. There is not enough space to testify of the countless interventions when God visited us. Miracles were frequent and unexplainable.

Revival and the breath of God would come upon that old tabernacle on Milldale's grounds over and over again. Genuine miracles, manifestations of God's presence, and an atmosphere that mortal tongue can not describe were the norm. Grounds filled with believers seeking the face of God, praying and crying out could be heard from down the street. The little prayer Chapel was filled day and night with intercessory prayer while meetings were being conducted. You just had to be there, and even then words would fail you.

And so, I dedicate this labor of love to a man that I have always loved deeply and count as my greatest influence for Christ and my father in the faith. For 15 years we lived and labored side by side and were inseparable. Unfortunate circumstances separated us from each other, but no amount of time could ever depreciate my love, respect and appreciation for this man of God. After 28 years, God has brought us back together. I will be forever thankful to the Lord for this reunion.

Pastor Jimmy Robertson, a man after God's own heart, I dedicate this book to you, my old friend.

# Table of Contents

# Acknowledgements

Writing my first novel has been a joy. But, as always, there are those who have partnered with me to make this story come to life:

Billie Kaye (my wife); she has always been faithful to honestly help guide my thinking. She has encouraged me to write this novel and has helped edit its contents.

Cynthia Watke; we have worked with her many times in the past. Her work in proofing, editing, organizing, and providing the book and cover design has been invaluable. She's gifted, talented and a blessing to work with.

Dr. J. Tod Zeiger has again added his own unique expertise to this offering. His extensive travel knowledge, along with biblical insights, have been a welcome addition to this project.

Mercury Press in Oklahoma City has been providing quality work for our ministry since 1991. Owners, Gary and Cheryl Wright, have been there for us time and time again. Jim Howlett, our boots on the ground at Mercury, always offers great assistance and timely coordination of our printing projects.

# Preface

Sometime in the early 90's I was speaking in a Bible conference and heard an illustration about the Kingdom of God being like a man seeking goodly pearls. For years I contemplated that story and with some imagination added to its contents. One evening in 2013 God stirred my heart to write this illustration in story form. I rushed to my office as thoughts and scenes unfolded in my mind. As I began typing, almost without thought, this story began to pour forth from my heart. Being a romantic at heart, I found myself lost in the story line almost as if I were there myself. There were sights, sounds, smells, people and places that came alive as I wrote.

I desire more than anything to communicate through this touching story the illustration I heard over 20 years ago. And so I offer to you, my readers, a novel rooted and grounded in the greatest truth God ever revealed to mortal man. I pray that you will be caught up in the story and overwhelmed by its message.

# CHAPTER ONE

## **An Innocent Question**

Outward appearances can be deceiving. They don't always tell the whole story.

Carl and Opal were affectionately known as Pawpaw and Mimi to family and friends. Children, grandchildren, many friends and several success-ful jewelry stores they established blessed their lives.

They met when they were in their late teens, fell in love and worked hard at their marriage. They reared three wonderful children and built a great future for the entire family. All their friends looked to them for advice in most matters that count in life. Having sold their stores to a well-known chain, they were enjoying the first year of their retirement. But, beneath a suc-cessful surface, there was something missing.

They felt an emptiness they couldn't explain. Like the feeling you have when you know something's wrong but you just can't put your finger on it. They felt a continual gnawing at their hearts. Carl and Opal had avoided talking about this emptiness for years, but both knew it was there. Once, when they were very young, they started to open up to each other about how unfulfilled they felt but life happened, and they never revisited their feelings.

But this night would be different. Old feelings would be brought to the surface, not by them, but by an innocent question. A question asked as they sat around the fireplace after a great Thanksgiving meal with all their children and grandchildren.

The question came in the form of a statement. "Pawpaw, isn't life just the greatest?" asked Meagan Ashley, their very special eight-year-old granddaughter, who was certainly Pawpaw's favorite. She was special not only because she was the oldest grandchild, but also because they almost lost her at birth and spent sleepless nights in worry and fear. She seemed the least likely to ask the question. They remembered the doctors telling them that unless there was a miracle she would never live past her teenage years. It was such an innocent question. No one knew it would open up a door that had been locked tight for many years.

Pawpaw slowly surveyed the room full of family with his precious wife of forty-three years. As tears filled his eyes, he replied, "Life is wonderful, my precious." As everyone was looking at their hero, they were shocked by what they heard next. For some strange reason Pawpaw choose that moment to talk about the void: the emptiness. As he began to open his heart to his family his wife joined in to validate his words.

An hour passed that seemed like only minutes as they both poured out their hearts to their wide-eyed, open-mouthed children and grandchildren. It was an evening no one would ever forget; an evening that began the greatest adventure of all for the elderly couple. Nothing had ever been able to fill that hole in their hearts: not a great family, close friends or success. Not even the admiration of all who knew them.

Late that night, after everyone was gone, Carl and Opal lay in bed looking at each other for a long time. When you've been married that long words aren't necessary. All of a sudden they both broke into a smile from ear to ear. As they reflected on the evening's revelations, they began to weep considering the adventure on which they were about to embark. The night was sleepless as they excitedly talked and settled it once and for all.

We're going to do this thing!

We're going to fulfill the secret unspoken dream we've had for years.

We're not going to stop until we've found *The Pearl of Great Price* we heard about a lifetime ago.

✠

That lifetime ago was the first few days of their honeymoon. Their parents had gifted them with a two-week vacation in Jamaica. How exciting it was for two kids who had never even visited other states, let alone traveled outside the country, to now be visiting another country on their honeymoon. Their arrival to this beautiful paradise was nothing short of magical. The sea, the sun and the whole atmosphere permeated their very souls. They had saved themselves for this first night and their expectations were only a shadow of the joy and love they experienced.

The first days of their honeymoon were nothing short of heavenly. They reveled in walks along the beautiful beaches of Ocho Rios with waves washing up to their ankles. They could only smile at each other over breakfast on the open deck overlooking the ocean. Those smiles turned into hours of talking together and dreaming of their future.

"What will our future look like?" they asked one another. "How many children will we have, and where will we be when we reach our parents' age?" they mused. The first two days were filled with a greater intimacy in every way than they ever thought possible.

On the morning of the third day is when the void appeared for the newlyweds.

The morning started like the first two: a precious morning greeting, a quiet breakfast and a walk along the beach. Near the end of the walk, a tall, lanky Jamaican appeared to be walking directly towards them. They tried to avoid eye contact with him as he grew closer, but it was impossible. There was something about the way he carried himself… the way his eyes seem to focus on them: eyes, that even from a distance, projected confidence and purpose.

Carl and Opal felt an unusual sense of peace and calm as he approached. Finally, face-to-face, stopping just short of each other, they spoke. "Morning," said the stranger. The couple responded at the same time, "Morning to you." Then the tall stranger reached inside an old worn burlap bag slung over his shoulder and pulled out two pieces of yellowish paper. Without a word, a piece of paper in both hands, he handed one to each of them. With a smile that would light up a room he simply said, "Have a blessed life," then turned and walked away.

The young couple watched him walk away and then turned and looked at each other with a "wasn't that nice" look on their face. Then, as if compelled by the paper in their hands, they both turned towards the ocean and lifted the paper to read. It was a hand-written note with no greeting or salutation; only a quote. As the sun beat down on their faces, the noise of the waves in their ears and the taste of salt in their mouth, they each quietly read the note handed to them. After what seemed like an eternity, they turned back toward each other and realized something had profoundly changed. For all their joy and excitement about the future, they were aware for the first time that there was something missing. Yes, they had each other and were going to spend their life together, but something was amiss.

Now they felt a sudden emptiness they didn't understand. As they walked along the beach in silence, questions flooded their minds.

Oceanside vendors hawked trinkets and memorabilia to tourists. One very noticeable man wore a walking billboard with messages on front and back. He was a large barrel-chested man with long, flowing blonde hair. The sign read, "VISIT G & F GIFT SHOP--TRASH OR TREASURE, YOU DECIDE." There was something about that man and his sign that caused them both to respond, "Let's go there soon." As so often occurs, time flew by and they did not visit the shop.

That was a most eventful day for the young couple. In the short exchange with the man on the beach, awareness was created. A subtle awareness that in their joy, there might still be something missing. This thought stayed with them all through the years. The years brought much happiness and fulfillment, to their marriage, and to them as individuals, but the message of the note handed to them on the beach never left them.

✠

This is the journey they committed to that Thanksgiving night: a journey that would take them around the world. You may wonder, what could be so life impacting in that small note that it would stay with them for so long? Why did the message grip their hearts? The note would seem innocent and very non-threatening to anyone who would read its content. But, the message of the note has the same power to grip any human heart; even yours. The note contained an ancient quote that has been passed down for generations. Dare to read it and ponder its great content and everything could change in your life. The note the stranger handed the newlyweds that day simply said, "The kingdom of heaven is like unto a merchant man, seeking goodly pearls: who when he had found one pearl of great price, went and sold all that he had, and bought it."

The day after Thanksgiving, Carl and Opal called the family together once again for a family conference. Everyone had their own idea of what this was all about. As the children, their spouses, and the grandchildren gathered in the great room, every eye was on Carl and Opal.

Was this going to be good news or bad? Why were their parents acting like teenagers in love? Finally, dad broke the silence. With a big grin on his face he said, "Your mom and I have decided to run away from home."

Everyone broke out in a sigh of relief that the announcement didn't involve the "C" word. The oldest son said jokingly, "What are you running away from?" They all laughed.

Then Opal said, "Children, you know we love you and the babies, but Dad and I have had a dream for years, and we're finally going to pursue it."

Now the youngest granddaughter, Kadie Jewel, spoke up, "But Mimi, you've always said your dream came true in your family." She was special, being the caboose, and she was also Pawpaw's favorite.

To this very special granddaughter, Mimi replied, "That's true Hon, but Pawpaw and I have also had another dream: a dream to find *The Pearl of Great Price* we read about on our honeymoon. And as fulfilling as our family dream has been, our other unfulfilled dream has left us both quite empty."

With that, the evening was long and filled with unanswered questions. Needless to say, as thrilled and excited as the parents were, the children left feeling very confused. All they knew was that two weeks from that night their mother and father planned to embark on a trip that would take them to many different countries and numerous cities over the coming years. After a few more tears and a lot more laughter, everyone went home to ponder what they had heard.

Carl and Opal fell into bed totally exhausted. Each gathered their thoughts and reflected about what was in front of them. Occasionally, the silence would be broken with a burst of laughter.

Finally Carl spoke up.

"How is it possible to be so exhausted and so excited all at the same time? I feel like a kid on Christmas Eve waiting for Santa Claus to arrive."

Opal propped up on one elbow, looked straight into Carl's eyes and said, "Okay, okay… stop laughing for a moment. I want to ask you a serious question."

"Sure, Sweetheart, fire away," smiled Carl.

"I know we are both excited right now, but you're

not going to change your mind, are you? I mean, this is something we're committed to, right?"

Carl pulled her toward him and wrapped his arms around her.

"Honey, this has been our unspoken dream for over forty-four years. There is a Pearl out there somewhere and we are going to find it. So yes, I am totally committed. As they say in poker, I'm 'all in'!"

Somewhere around 4 a.m. sleep made a brief visit.

# CHAPTER TWO

## An Exciting Departure

Departure day came all too quickly for the children, but all too slowly for Mom and Dad. For the next two weeks Carl and Opal were extremely busy. Each night after dinner they sat in front of the computer and planned their itinerary. Because Carl had a background in the jewelry business, he had some idea of where he wanted to go to search for *The Pearl of Great Price*.

After spending several hours researching each day, Carl and Opal would sit together on the front porch just talking about things to come. But, this night was different; it was just a few days before their departure.

"Honey, I think we're ready. First stop, Hyderabad, India."

Opal did not know whether to laugh or cry, because that seemed such a long way from home.

"Sweetheart, why are we going such a long distance just to find a pearl? I thought we might start some place a little bit closer to home. But, I've trusted you for the last 44 years, and I trust you now. If you say that's where we need to start our search, then let's go to the travel agency tomorrow morning and purchase our tickets."

Carl laughed, "I did that days ago."

The exciting day finally arrived. Tickets in hand and luggage for their journey, their children reluctantly drove them to the International Terminal. Their family had all thought at some point Mom and Dad would come to their senses and realize that such a trip at their age was just a waste of time. It's not that they didn't want them to be excited or have fun in their golden years; it's just that life was not going to be the same without them. Their parents were the constant in their lives. They could always count on Papaw and Mimi to be there when needed.

The send off was a sight to behold. Grandchildren were thinking how cool it was for Mimi and Pawpaw to be running away from home. Children were trying one last time to reason with their parents. But, Carl and Opal would not be moved. It took all the restraint they had not to laugh aloud because of the excitement they felt.

When the attendant announced First Class boarding, they turned to their family and assured them, "Don't worry about us, this is our dream come true. We love you all very much. We will be back before you know it."

With that they turned and boarded their flight for the first stop of their journey, Hyderabad, India.

Soon after embarking, the flight attendant walked by making sure everyone in first class was settled comfortably in their seats. She was offering complimentary drinks when Carl stopped her.

"Excuse me, Ma'am, could you tell me the flying time to Hyderabad?"

"Yes sir, of course. It is just a smidgen over 16 hours."

Carl squeezed Opal's hand. "Don't worry Honey, it'll go by fast. We will have plenty of time to relax, watch a movie or two, take a nap, and before you know it, we will be there."

After a lovely meal, they pushed back in their seats to enjoy a nice nap. Suddenly, Carl felt a slight tug on his arm, opened his eyes and noticed a flight attendant staring at him.

"Sorry to bother you sir, but normally about halfway in our flight we offer some very exciting items to purchase in our in-flight catalog. When you get a minute, take a look at the catalog and let me know if you find anything you would like to purchase."

Carl didn't have the heart to wake up Opal just yet so he waited a bit longer. While he was waiting he flipped through the catalog and dog-eared a few pages he wanted her to look at. There are certain perks passengers enjoy when sitting in first class that you don't find in coach: excellent food and purchasing items from an exclusive catalog, just to name a couple perks.

A little later, after Opal awakened, they started flipping through the catalog together.

Before they got very far, the flight attendant came back and looked straight into Carl's eyes.

"I know what you're looking for, but you won't find it in the catalog."

Opal leaned over and whispered in Carl's ear, "Did she say what I thought she just said?"

Instead of answering Opal's question he looked at the flight attendant and asked, "What are you talking about? How do you know what we are looking for?"

Carl was not much for mysteries or anything that could not be explained. So he asked her again, "How could you possibly know what we're looking for?"

It seemed the demeanor of the flight attendant changed in an instant. With a mysterious look she said in low voice, "I know you're looking for pearls, but you won't find them in the catalog. If you are interested, let me bring you a sample of some of the finest pearls in the world, and then you decide if the trip is really worth it."

By this time Carl and Opal were both a little concerned. Did she overhear them discussing their journey to find *The Pearl of Great Price*? How did she know so much about their personal business?

Pushing the mystery aside, Carl told the flight attendant to show him what she had.

Carl turned to Opal, "Of course, honey, you know if we can find it here on the plane, of all places, we can enjoy our time in Hyderabad, buy a few souvenirs and head back home."

"Well, I guess it won't hurt to look at what she has, but I don't see any way we are going to find what we are looking for on the plane."

After a few minutes the flight attendant returned holding a small tray.

"Here, take a look at these. Aren't they beautiful?"

"Yes, I must say they are very lovely. Why don't you give us a few minutes to look through what you have, and we will let you know if we want to buy one or two."

As Carl and Opal looked at the small tray of pearls, they suspected these were not the pearls for which they were searching. Somehow they believed in their hearts when they found that one special pearl it would mysteriously fill their emptiness.

As they continued looking at the pearls another unusual thing happened.

"I don't mean to interrupt," said the stranger sitting directly across the aisle from Carl. "I couldn't help but overhear your conversation with the flight attendant. Please, let me introduce myself. My name is Henry Smith, and I have been in the jewelry business for over 50 years. Do you mind if I take a look?"

By this time Carl was thinking to himself, "How in the world do all these people know our business? Are we that obvious?"

"No, sir, I do not mind at all. I've been in the jewelry business for years too, but I didn't think to bring along my jeweler's loop on this trip. If you have yours along, why don't you take a look at this exceptional pearl I took from the tray. I think I might buy this one."

Henry studied the pearl for a few minutes. He reached inside his coat pocket and pulled out his jeweler's loop. He studied the pearl from every angle.

"Do you know what you have here?"

"Not really, I just know it is a beautiful specimen," said Carl.

"I don't mean to burst your bubble, but what you have here are commonly referred to as Majorca pearls. These pearls are from Majorca, Spain and are made to look like the real thing. You can go into most department stores and find these. All sorts of jewelry are made from these pearls, including earrings and necklaces. They are made in a factory, not in the ocean. In other words, they are fake, or as we say in the business, faux pearls. To the untrained eye it can be deceiving. A lot of women wear faux pearls. There's nothing wrong with that as long as you know what you're buying. My advice to you, sir, is never settle for a substitute when you're looking for the real thing!"

Just then, the flight attendant returned. "So, how many of these beautiful pearls would you like to purchase?"

Carl handed the tray back to the flight attendant.

"No, thank you, we have decided to search for the real thing and not settle for a substitute."

The flight attendant looked agitated. "Are you sure? I can give you a great price. You can save money, time and effort. Why wouldn't you want a deal like that?"

Carl did not want to sound rude, and he was yet to figure out why the flight attendant was so interested in what they were doing.

"Yes, we're very sure.  We'll just wait until we find exactly what we're looking for," said a disappointed Carl.

✠

As the plane slowly descended, the lights of Hyderabad came into view. Carl had picked up brochures from the travel agency of all of the cities they planned to visit. He thought it would be a good idea before they landed to read up on the city called *The City of Pearls*.

Landing at Hyderabad's new Rajiv Gandhi International Airport was a phenomenal experience.  Carl and Opal thought the airport would be old and decrepit; instead they found a modern up-to-date facility. After going through passport control and customs, they decided to take the option of riding in an air-conditioned bus afforded by the airport, to their hotel. Checking in was easy. They were relieved to follow the young Indian, who worked for the concierge service, to the room. They thanked him as he placed their luggage on the floor.

He said, "Is there anything else you would require? It is the desire of the staff of the hotel to make your stay as pleasant as possible."

Carl handed him a five-dollar tip.

"No, I can't think of anything right now, but thank you for your kindness."

As the bellman started to leave, he stopped at the door and looked at Carl and Opal. "I do hope you find what you're looking for."

Carl couldn't take another mystery.

"How do you know we're looking for something?"

"Oh, just a hunch. Usually people who come here from the West are looking for something, and I have an idea that you two are no different. Anyway, I hope you have a restful time. Good luck."

Tired and weary from the trip, they decided to sleep, hoping to be refreshed for their search the next day.

The next morning Carl and Opal ordered room service and mapped out their strategy for the day. Munching on a piece of toast, Carl studied a map of the city that he had picked up in the lobby while checking in. On the last page of the brochure he found a list of recommended stores and shops. One recommendation stood out above the rest. His eyes locked on to one particular store that advertised, *Your first and last stop to buy the most beautiful pearls in India.*

He could hardly contain his excitement. "Look, sweetheart, I think I found the place we need to go."

"Okay, you're the navigator, lead the way."

Even though they had mapped out an itinerary that would literally take them around the world, they both hoped the first stop would bring them success. *The Pearl* they read about so many years before would be in their possession, and they could go home and spend the remainder of their years loving and enjoying their children and grandchildren. They were willing, of course, to take as much time as needed. Words did not have to be spoken, because they both knew time was against them. With each passing year the hunger in their hearts had not decreased but only intensified.

✠

While Carl waited for Opal to finish drying her hair and to put the last touches on her makeup, his mind began to wander back to when he was a boy. For some strange reason he started thinking about a day that he was playing marbles in the front yard with some of his friends. He was maybe eight or nine years old. Oh, how he loved marbles. He had the best collection of marbles in the neighborhood, and everybody knew him as the "marble master."

One day while playing with some of his buddies, a group of older boys walked by and stopped to watch the master at work.

"Hey kid, we're headed down to the park to play baseball and we need one more. You interested?" asked one of the older boys.

"Sure thing," said Carl, "I guess I can take a break and help you boys out."

That was the day that Carl fell in love with baseball. He sold his collection of marbles and saved up enough money to buy a new glove, ball and bat. It was only sometime later that young Carl realized that his desire to play marbles had been supplanted by a new love: baseball.

There are times in life when you're offered an opportunity to give up something you love for something greater. While sitting there, it dawned on Carl that maybe this was what this search was all about. He was ready to trade in his marbles for baseball.

No one knows what motivates people. For some, it is money and the abundance of 'things'. For others, it is power and the ability to control and manipulate other people. No matter the motivation, everyone has desires and unfulfilled dreams. Carl and Opal were no exception. A successful business and wonderful children and grandchildren were not substitutes for something missing in their hearts.

"We have no idea what is to come. There may be plenty of opportunities for substitutes, shortcuts, and taking the easy way out. We cannot fathom the number of distractions that might be thrown at us. Yet, through it all, we will not be deterred until we exhaust all our resources, and if necessary, even our own lives, to find *The Pearl of Great Price!*" thought Carl.

"Are you about ready, sweetheart? I called for a taxi. I'm sure he's downstairs waiting on us. Time to get moving."

# CHAPTER THREE

## An Empty
## Pursuit

Carl and Opal jumped into the back of the taxi. Carl handed the driver a piece of paper with the address of the shop.

"Oh yes, I know this place. I will take you there straightaway," said the taxi driver.

Carl had traveled overseas before, but this was Opal's first trip. The trip from the hotel to the jewelry store felt like taking your life into your own hands. It was a culture shock. She marveled at how people could live in such conditions. The smell, the sounds, and the weird traffic patterns were enough to put even the bravest souls into a state of panic.

They made it unharmed and in one piece thanks to a skilled taxi driver who was used to dodging traffic and certain members of the bovine family.

"Welcome, welcome to my shop. My name is Reyansh, and I am the owner of this fine establishment. I am at your service. What can I do to help my American friends? I know what you're looking for, and I have just the thing for you. Yes, yes, you're looking for pearls, and you have come to the right place."

Carl and Opal looked at each other and immediately knew what each other was thinking. "He knows we are American, and he knows we're looking for pearls. At some point were going to have to figure out what is giving us away!"

They both decided to talk about it later, but for now it was time to find the *Perfect Pearl*.

Reyansh was a slightly built man in his late 50s. Along with his older brother Dandak, he had founded Jagdamba Pearls over 20 years before. They established a reputation for fine quality pearls at very affordable prices. It was not uncommon to see the rich and famous frequent their shop. A quick glance around the walls and you would likely see a picture of a Saudi prince or someone of British royalty. If you weren't sure who they were, Reyansh was more than happy to spend an hour telling you about all the expensive pearls he sold them.

Carl found it difficult to explain exactly what he was looking for. After all, how do you ask for *The Pearl of Great Price*?

After a few more complementary words about how much he loved America, Reyansh spoke up and said, "Now, what can I show you?"

Carl tried to explain their quest the best he could.

"I may not be able to explain it exactly right, but we will know it when we see it. So, if you don't mind, please just show us what you have available."

Reyansh disappeared into the back room and after a short time reappeared behind the counter holding two trays of pearls.

"Look! Look at what I have. I think there is something here that you might be interested in. Take your time. When you have found something you like let me know and I will give you a good price."

While Carl and Opal were fingering through the tray of pearls a young man walked over and stood next to them. He had been standing at the end of the counter listening to their conversation. At first they felt a little uncomfortable, but he seemed harmless: more interested in looking at the pearls than anything else. The young man finally broke the silence.

"Sir, I could not help but overhear your conversation with Reyansh. I have been coming to this shop for many years, and I can tell you that you won't find better pearls in all of India than what you hold in your hand. But, I must ask you, exactly what are you looking for?"

The last thing Carl and Opal wanted to do was engage in conversation with this stranger. After all, it was none of his business why they were in the shop. Carl thought, "If I give away too many details about what we're doing we could find *The Pearl*, and before we get back to the hotel someone may mug us and take it away from us."

"Sir, if you don't mind, my wife and I would like to spend some time looking through these two trays and be on our way."

"No problem," said the stranger, "I will leave you to your business. I just want to tell you one last thing. What you are looking for will never be found in a pearl. Physical things will never satisfy the hunger in your heart. And, by the way, never settle for a substitute in place of what you really want."

Now Carl felt really agitated. He wanted to offer a rebuttal to the stranger, but the last thing he wanted was an argument with someone he'd never met in a country to which he's never been. He thought it best just to let the man walk away and get back to the business of finding *The Pearl*.

Opal waited for the man to walk out the door.

"Honey, haven't we heard that advice before?"

"Yes, dear, it's the same thing the man on the plane said, remember?"

"Yes, I remember now. How is it possible that two men we had never met gave us the same advice?"

"Sweetheart, it's beyond my comprehension at the moment. I don't know how that is possible. All I know is that we are on a journey to find something that we are missing. We are not going to stop until we find it. Now, let's get back to business."

Carl and Opal spent most of the morning looking through the inventory of pearls. Occasionally they would stop and examine one that struck their fancy, but it just didn't feel right. In between helping other customers Reyansh would walk over and ask Carl if he found anything that might interest him.

"Remember, don't hesitate! When you find something let me know. I'm here to help you," said Reyansh.

Finally Carl turned to Opal, "Honey, I don't know what to say. We have been here all morning. I think we have looked through every tray of pearls in the shop.

Maybe the best thing for us to do is to go back to the hotel and regroup."

Opal agreed that maybe it was a good time to have lunch, rest and think about their next step.

Reyansh did everything possible to find them just the right pearl. He was determined to make his new American friends happy and was willing to do anything possible, including offering them a generous discount. When it was all said and done, Carl and Opal gave up the search for the day and headed back to the hotel.

✠

Waking up from a late afternoon nap, Carl had an overwhelming sense of gloom. He didn't know what was going on. All he knew was the emptiness he felt in his heart was like a gathering fog that shrouded everything, including his thoughts.

Sipping on a cup of hot tea, trying to get fully awake, he did a few mental gymnastics to shake away the fog. He kept reminding himself that he and Opal were on a mission, and they were not going to be deterred after visiting one shop.

A delicious supper, a quiet evening, a hot shower and it was off to bed. Carl thought, "Maybe tomorrow will bring success. I don't plan on giving up." With that thought in mind, Carl drifted off to sleep.

The next morning Carl was up bright and early. He thought it best to let Opal sleep in. After all, it's hard to get over jet lag in one day. He was headed for the door to see if the morning paper had arrived when he noticed a note lying on the floor. Sometime during the night someone had placed it under the door.

Cautiously, he opened the note and read, "I know what you're looking for. Meet me on the eastern side street, adjacent to the hotel." There was no signature.

Carl gently tugged on Opal's shoulder. "Honey, I'm going to go downstairs and grab a little breakfast. I'll give you a ring in a couple of hours to see if you want me to bring you something to eat."

He didn't want to alarm her or cause her undue worry. He thought he would just go and see what the note was all about. The urgency he felt to find *The Pearl* was so strong he didn't realize that he could be headed for grave trouble.

He left the hotel and turned right on to the adjacent street. Sitting tucked a little back into an alleyway was a black Mercedes with very dark windows... so dark you could not see inside.

Carl was very nervous. Under normal conditions he would never do this. While he stared at the Mercedes, the back window rolled down, and he heard a voice.

"Come closer, my friend, I need to talk to you."

Carl inched his way closer but not too close, for after all, he did not know whether this person was friend or foe.

Meanwhile, in the hotel room, Opal opened her eyes and looked at the clock. The best she could tell it had been over an hour since Carl left for breakfast. She desperately wanted to tell him about the dream. It was one of those dreams, almost a nightmare, that when you're having it you can't tell if it's real or not.

She kept staring at the room phone hoping Carl would call soon, because she felt like she needed to warn him. She didn't know what was going on. All she knew was that in her dream she saw a dark figure talking to Carl, and there was something about the figure that felt all wrong. Call it intuition or premonition – she felt he could be in danger.

"Drive with me, my friend. I am going to take you to the most wonderful place to help you find what you're looking for," said the stranger.

Carl decided that he was not going anywhere with a stranger just yet.

"How do you know what I'm looking for?"

The stranger peered through the small crack in the window. "I know you Americans come here looking for pearls. After all, it's called *The City of Pearls* for a reason. Everyone wants a deal, and I am the one person in Hyderabad that can make you a deal of a lifetime. So, if you're ready to find the most beautiful pearl in all of India, get in the car."

Carl couldn't believe he was actually getting in the car, but something told him this might be the answer. The car sped away through the back streets and back alleys of Hyderabad. Finally, after a drive that seemed to take forever, they pulled up in front of a small building with a sign above the door: East India Imports/Exports Shop.

The stranger said, "This is the place, my friend."

As they exited the car he ushered Carl into the front of the store. It was a very small room: dark and dingy. It did not look like the kind of shop that was open to the public. There was trash on the floor and boxes stacked everywhere. As Carl surveyed the room, he did notice a small jewelry counter on the opposite end of the shop.

"Please forgive my manners. My name is Danu Negas. I have been in the Import/Export business for many years. Excuse the mess; I've been away on business."

"No problem, I owned several jewelry stores myself, so I know that things can pile up. My wife and I are on a journey to find a certain kind of pearl. I'm not sure you have what we are looking for, but I'm willing to see what you have."

Back at the hotel two hours had passed, and still no word from Carl. Opal was in a panic. "Where could he have gone? Did he go for a walk to look around the city? Where is he? Why doesn't he call?" She paced the room, sat down a while and then paced some more. She felt such an urgency. She had to find him. She had to get in touch with him and tell him about her dream. She had to warn him.

The dark stranger was a man of few words. He told Carl he was going into the back to bring out a few items for him to look at. It suddenly dawned on Carl that he had been gone from the hotel for a while. How he hoped that Opal was still asleep so that she wouldn't worry.

He glanced up and the man standing behind the counter beckoned him to come over and take a look. Carl walked over as Mr. Negas placed a number of pearls on a black velvet cloth on the counter in front of him.

What a display it was! It seemed that there were pearls from the four corners of the earth: Persian Gulf Pearls, Conch Pearls, Quahog Pearls, Antique Naturals, Clam Pearls, and Melo Pearls. Carl was amazed. He had not seen anything like this the day before.

"Sir, you have an amazing collection. The brilliance alone is enough to hurt my eyes. Where did you get all of these?"

"You cannot imagine the time and effort it took to collect all of these from around the world. I'm sure there's something here you might be interested in. Whatever you do, don't pass up this opportunity. It only comes around once in a lifetime," said the stranger with a slight grin on his face.

After about an hour of looking, Carl focused his attention on a particularly beautiful Persian Gulf Pearl. Even though he did not feel that this particular pearl was the one, *The Pearl,* at least he could get Opal's opinion before going any further.

"Oh, I was hoping you would focus on that one. It's one of my all-time favorites. I can make you a great price, if you buy it today."

"I appreciate the offer, but before you give me a price I need to talk to my wife and bring her back with me, because I would never make a decision without her."

"No! You have to make a decision now. The price will go up if you delay. I'm sure your wife would approve, and after all, what a surprise it's going to be when you go back and show her what you bought."

But Carl was emphatic. "We're on this journey together, and I would never think of doing anything without her input. So, if you don't mind, have your driver take me back to the hotel, and I will bring her back here in just a few hours."

Finally, the stranger agreed for his driver to take Carl back to the hotel. He told Carl the driver would not be able to wait for him.

"Just give the address to any taxi driver. They can find my shop with no problem. But, I'm going to warn you, I cannot promise the same deal later that I'm willing to give you now. The best thing is to go ahead and make a decision and not worry about your wife. Surely you can make a decision by yourself."

Carl felt an unusual temptation to make a decision even though he knew in his heart it would probably be wrong. The last thing he wanted to do was disappoint Opal; on the other hand, he was tempted to take a chance. After a few more minutes of his mind playing good cop-bad cop, he finally answered the stranger.

"No, take me back to the hotel now. I don't feel comfortable having this conversation any longer."

Opal heard the door open to their room and ran to meet Carl as he walked through the door. "I have been worried sick. Are you all right? Are you hurt? Were you kidnapped? Why didn't you call me? It's been over three hours!"

Carl didn't know which question to answer first.

"Hold on Honey, I'm fine. I'm sorry I didn't call you, but I didn't have access to a phone. I had the most unusual experience."

Before Carl could go any further with his strange tale, Opal interrupted him.

"Before you tell me anymore, I need to tell you about the dream I had. I dreamed that you had a conversation with a dark figure, and this figure was trying to get you to do something you didn't really want to do. I can't really explain it. The only thing I know to say is, you were about to compromise everything, and I woke up from the dream with the urgency to warn you."

Opal burst into tears. "But you were gone, and I was so worried because I couldn't warn you."

Finally she composed herself.

"Now, Carl, please tell me what happened."

After giving her details of the past three hours, they both agreed that the dream was somehow connected to his experience with the dark stranger.

"Honey, I'm not discounting your dream, but I feel that I need to take you back and at least let you look at the same pearl I saw. I'm not sure it is *The Pearl* we are seeking, but at least we need to look at it and make a decision together."

✠

After a quick lunch, they hailed a taxi. Carl handed a piece of paper with the address of the East India Imports/Exports Shop to the taxi driver. As they dodged traffic, Carl continued to fill in the details about his experience.

The driver pulled over to the curb and said, "Sir, this is the address."

Carl asked the taxi driver to wait while he and Opal got out to go into the shop. As they stepped inside the door, Carl knew something was radically different. The sign of the export shop was gone; a different sign was in its place. Inside he looked around the shop and all he saw were computers and several sales clerks.

"Good afternoon, Sir, may we help you?"

"Is this not the East India Imports/Exports Shop?"

"Oh no, sir, this is Abacus Computer Services."

Carl turned around and walked out the door. He looked up again at the sign above the door. Sure enough it read Abacus Computer Service.

Carl was not about to pay the taxi driver for taking

them to the wrong address. He leaned in the window and asked the taxi driver, "Are you sure this is the right address? This is not the shop I was in only a couple hours ago."

"Sir, this is the address you gave me. I have been driving in this city for 10 years, and I know my way around. If you would like, I will call my dispatcher and ask him for the correct address of the East India Imports/Exports Shop. Obviously, the name of the shop and the address do not match."

The taxi driver called his dispatcher and waited for an answer. After a few minutes the dispatcher called back. "There is no address found in our directory for the East India Imports/Exports Shop. As far as I know, there has never been a business by that name. You must tell your passengers they are mistaken."

Carl was clearly upset and confused. He instructed the taxi driver to take them back to the hotel. He was determined to get to the bottom of this. It's not that he didn't believe the dispatcher; after all, there was no reason to lie, but he wanted another opinion.

When they got back to the hotel, he went directly to the desk clerk.

"Can you help me? I need to check on the address for a particular business."

"Yes, of course. Just give me the name of the business and the address you have."

Carl and Opal settled in the tearoom and waited for an answer. Finally, the desk clerk came over.

"Sir, I have had two operators looking for the business at the address you gave me, and they assure me that no such business exists in all of Hyderabad."

The rest of the evening was awkward, to say the least. Carl kept trying to explain that his experience was real. Opal kept asking questions, trying to understand where he had been for over three hours and what had caused him to make such a risky trip. Finally, they agreed to get a good night's sleep and talk about it in the morning.

The next morning, over breakfast, they continued their conversation about the unusual experiences of the day before. They decided Carl's experience was a mystery. It was clearly real, but the warning Opal received in her dream was also real. They both realized how close they had come to grave danger, in addition to making a rash purchase decision.

After several more days in Hyderabad of looking and not finding *The Pearl*, they decided it was time to continue their search elsewhere. The last few nights of their stay were spent looking over brochures they had brought along from home with pictures of their next destination.

They felt disappointed that they had not found *The Pearl* but thankful that the mysterious experience had not resulted in loss of life or a purchasing decision they might both regret.

# CHAPTER FOUR

## An Overwhelming Frustration

The jumbo jet slowly descended through the clouds. Carl and Opal could see the bright lights of the city of Broome, Western Australia. Flying from Hyderabad to the coast of Western Australia was an easy decision to make. Although it was a long trip, they felt it was going to be worth it. Through his research Carl had discovered that on the West Coast of Australia pearls were almost an obsession, especially around the coastal area of Roebuck Bay.

There was a huge contrast between where they had been and where they were going. Hyderabad is a city of over 7 million compared to Broome which is a city of only 14,000, swelling to over 45,000 during the tourist season. Not only was there a population difference but there was also a cultural difference. Carl and Opal both felt more at home and at ease, because it was easier to communicate with the locals.

Broome is a favorite destination for backpackers looking for pearling work. It also produces some of the best pearls in the world. There was no doubt in their mind they had come to the right place to find *The Pearl of Great Price*.

Staying at the Pearle Resort on the beach had its perks. Not only did the five-star hotel offer a free shuttle from Broome International Airport, the ocean view combined with all the amenities offered was more than they could ever hope for. The Pearle was built to represent a little paradise of Bali. Of course, they had to remember the reason why they were there. On more than one occasion during their visit to Broome they had to remind each other to keep their eye on the prize. Finding *The Pearl* was priority number one. A little sightseeing and relaxing on the beach was just a byproduct.

They were both up early the next morning full of anticipation. Having their breakfast out on the veranda overlooking the ocean reminded them of the time they spent at Ocho Rios on their honeymoon.

As the sun was rising above the horizon Opal looked at Carl.

"Honey, do you remember that first morning in Ocho Rios when we had breakfast out on the veranda? Does this remind you of that?"

Carl could feel the fire of love in his heart rekindling for Opal as she talked. There were times he took her for granted, but today his heart was stirred by the memory of his lovely bride.

"Yes, Hon, I do remember. We have come a long way. It's been a long journey with a lot of ups and downs, but I could not have picked a better partner for the journey than you."

Carl put down his fork. He leaned over and gave her a kiss.

"Let's find *The Pearl* and complete our journey together."

Opal wiped away a glimmer of tear in her eye.

"Honey, you are the most wonderful man I've ever known. I have loved you from the moment I laid eyes on you. Somehow. I believe finding *The Pearl* we heard about so many years ago will bring the added fulfillment to our lives that we have desperately needed."

For about an hour they sat, talked, and laughed as they planned their itinerary for the day. They decided the first stop would be Linneys' Pearl Shop.

Walking through the door of Linneys' was an experience beyond words: pearls, pearls and more pearls. They had everything. If you could put a pearl in it, on it, or around it, they had it. They decided this time not to engage a salesman but simply to look around. Every time a salesperson came up and asked if they could help them they would simply say, "No, thank you, we are just looking."

Without saying a word they quickly concluded this was not the place to find *The Pearl*. Not to take away from the beauty of the merchandise, there was just something about the atmosphere and the merchandise that told them, "Not here, keep moving on."

After another hour of looking around, they decided to move on to the next stop on their itinerary: Willie Creek Pearls.

They were informed at the hotel the best way to get there was to wait for the bus to take them. After an hour or so of waiting, a bus finally pulled up in front and a man named Gary opened the door.

"Next stop, Willie Creek Pearl Farm, hop on."

Of course he had to make all the rounds of area hotels picking up more passengers before making the 25 km trip. The rough roads didn't matter to Carl and Opal, because Gary entertained them by sharing his deep knowledge about the pearl industry.

When they arrived at the Willie Creek Pearl Farm, an Englishman named Daniel gave an interesting and very entertaining classroom type lecture on how pearls are produced. Then they took a short boat trip into the actual creek. It was one of the highest tides they'd had for months; needless to say, it was great fun. The staff showed Carl and Opal how to clean all the shells on the long lines. Following the hands-on experience, they enjoyed tea, coffee, and homemade cakes.

Suddenly they realized the afternoon was almost gone. They decided to go back to the shop and see if they could find what they were looking for by trying a new approach. They would split up and double their efforts.

A little later Opal looked across the room at Carl standing with one of the sales people showing him a tray of pearls. He had the most unusual look on his face. "What could be happening now?" she asked herself.

As she caught up with Carl, she said, "Honey, are you all right?"

He didn't answer but brushed past her to ask another clerk to show him another tray of pearls. Opal was shocked. This was not like her husband, so putting her hand on his shoulder, she faced him, looked him directly in the eye, and said, "My dear, what is wrong?"

Without so much as a word of warning the dam of Carl's frustration broke through… "I CAN'T TAKE THIS ANYMORE! DO YOU REALIZE HOW MANY THOUSANDS OF MILES WE HAVE TRAVELED AND HOW MUCH MONEY WE HAVE SPENT TO FIND THE SO-CALLED PEARL OF GREAT PRICE? I DON'T WANT TO KNOW HOW CULTURED PEARLS ARE MADE, OR WHEN THE PEARLING INDUS-TRY STARTED, OR HOW MANY ABORIGINES DIED TRYING TO HARVEST PEARLS…THIS IS JUST ENOUGH!"

In all the years of marriage, Opal had never seen Carl like this. She could understand his frustration with the search, but her shock showed in her face as she pled, "Honey, please lower your voice. People are beginning to stare. Let's go into the courtyard and have a seat and talk this out."

She led the way into the courtyard and they sat down together. After a few minutes of awkward silence, Carl finally spoke.

"I am so sorry for the outburst, but my frustration level has reached the boiling point."

Carl reached in his pocket and pulled out a piece of paper with that day's itinerary written on it.

"Look, we're supposed to go to Paspaley's Pearls after this, but I don't think I have the heart or the desire to stand there and look at more pearls. Do you realize that if you combine all the pearls we've looked at from Hyderabad to Broome it would be several million dollars' worth, and still we can't find *The Pearl*? What is it going to take? Tell me? Come on, tell me what you think. I know you have an opinion; I want to hear it." His voice began to rise once again.

Opal decided to let him finish and get it all out of his system before answering. She knew it took a lot for him to share his real feelings, and she did not want to interrupt.

"Carl, do you really want to know what I think?"

"Yes, of course I do, or I wouldn't have asked," blurted her flustered husband.

"Well, first of all, Sweetheart, I am not your problem, so I would appreciate the next time you want to have a major meltdown in a public establishment to please give me a little warning. Carl, dear, you know that nothing has changed from the night we made the decision to go on this journey till now. We can't help it that so far we've not had any success, but remember why we are here.

You are not the only one frustrated; I am too, but I believe that this journey is the most important thing we will ever do with our lives. I don't believe we should stop until we find what we're looking for. Please remember that we both agreed that we would do anything to find *The Pearl of Great Price*, so let's regroup, take some time for ourselves, and maybe very soon we will have the energy to go back to the search, and make this *Pearl* ours."

Nothing like someone crashing your pity party! Opal's words hit their mark and shook Carl out of his gloom and doom attitude.

"You're right, Honey, please forgive me. I guess I'm just tired, but that is no excuse to have a meltdown. Why don't we go back to the hotel and put off going to Paspaley's to another day? We always have tomorrow."

☩

For three more long months they searched. Disappointing day after disappointing day, they kept searching. When one was discouraged and ready to quit, the other rallied and bolstered their courage to keep going. Utilizing Broome as their home base, they traveled to every imaginable spot in the Eastern Hemisphere hoping to find what they were looking for. Even though they both agreed that their visits to such exotic places were beautiful and exciting, they still could not hide their disappointment at the fruitlessness of their search.

Early one morning, the brilliant sun rising on a new day, they sat down to breakfast on the veranda of their hotel to talk about their next step.

As they were finishing up, Carl said to Opal, "I think I'm going to take a walk this morning and clear my head and do some serious thinking."

Opal jumped out of the chair as if she had been shot out of a cannon.

"Oh, no you don't! You're not going to leave me like you did in Hyderabad!"

"Sweetheart, believe me, I will never do that to you again. If you look on the counter in the kitchen you will see the two cell phones we rented at the airport upon arriving the other day. Remember? It was right after we passed through customs. I will take one, and you keep the other. I wrote the numbers on a piece of paper lying right beside the cell phones. If you need to reach me you can call me. It's not that I don't want you to go with me, but I just need some alone time with my thoughts. I'm sure you understand."

Opal knew that for both of them time alone had been rare during this journey. "Okay, I trust you, but please be careful, and don't be gone too long, promise?"

"Yes, dear, I promise."

Carl walked out of the lobby, turned right and found himself walking down a narrow path leading to the beach. The smell of saltwater and the sun creeping up over the horizon gave him a renewed sense of hope. As he got closer to the beach, he noticed an old wooden sign about to fall over that read, "CAPT. DAVE'S PEARL SHOP – IF WE CAN'T GET IT– YOU DIDN'T NEED IT ANYWAY."

Carl went in the general direction of the arrow on the bottom of the sign just to see what the pearl shop looked like. After walking over a small sand dune, he came upon a little shack with what looked like an old dinghy bobbing in the surf in front of it. Carl thought, "That thing has been through one too many storms."

He was just about to turn and walk away toward the beach when he heard a voice saying, "G-Day Mate, come on in."

Standing in the doorway was what could only be described as a real life pirate.

"Capt. Dave is my name. What can I do you for?"

Carl wanted to burst out laughing, because the only pirate he had ever seen was in the movies, and this guy looked like he just stepped off the soundstage. He had it all, including a patch over his right eye, and believe it or not, a parrot sitting on his shoulder. Carl thought he would play along, because after all, this was probably just an act for the tourist.

"Well, hello Capt. Dave, my name is Carl. Do you mind if I come in and look around your little shop?"

Carl walked through the door and approached this unusual character. He looked around the little shop and did not notice anything of significance.

Trying not to stare, he asked Capt. Dave, "So, how long have you been in business?"

Capt. Dave stared back at him and apparently didn't think his question was too important, because he never answered it.

"I know what you're looking for, Matey, and I'm just the man to find it for you."

Carl has heard this routine before, so he decided to play along.

"Well, I'm looking for a certain kind of pearl. Do you think you might be able to help me find it?"

Capt. Dave just kept staring at him.

Finally he said, "I will do better than that, Mate. I will guide you to find it. Give me a day, and if I don't take you to find the most beautiful pearl in all of the

South Sea, I will give you the cost of the boat rental plus buy your dinner. Now, how are you going to beat a deal like that? Are you in, or are you out?"

Carl pondered his options. He could graciously decline the offer, go back to the hotel, pick up Opal and visit more shops. Or, he could take a risk, accept the invitation, and see where it might lead.

"I'm in, now what?"

Capt. Dave let out a big laugh.

"Somehow, I knew you would be. You look like the adventurous type. Meet me at 6 AM tomorrow at dock number 12 in Roebuck Bay. Bring your wife along, if you want. You can take a taxi from the hotel. It will take you about an hour. If you are not on board by 6:05 AM the boat will be gone and your opportunity will be lost. I am too old to play games and too ornery to sit around and wait for you!"

Carl said goodbye and headed back toward the hotel. He was almost to the front door of the lobby when his cell phone rang. It was Opal calling to check on him.

"Yes, honey, I'm alright. I'll be there in a few minutes."

Carl explained his meeting with Capt. Dave and to his surprise Opal was excited about the possibility.

Based on past experience, Carl knew Opal was normally reluctant to try new things. Her famous statement
was always, "I just need time to process new informa-
tion," and with that any discussion about trying something new or adventurous would end. He was pleased
that she wanted to accompany him on the boat trip the
following morning.

The taxi ride to Roebuck Bay was a familiar one.
Over the last several months they'd taken the trip several times, exploring every shop along the way, looking
for that one special pearl.

"Ahoy, Matey, welcome aboard the Jewel of the Sea,"
bellowed Capt. Dave.

"Ahoy, yourself, Capt. Dave, we are reporting for
duty," said Carl with a big grin on his face.

Carl helped Opal onto the boat, squeezing her hand
while whispering in her ear, "Do your best not to laugh.
This guy thinks he's a pirate."

Sure enough, there he stood grinning from ear to
ear looking like he just walked out of the 1600s. "Find
some room, make yourself comfortable if you can. We
will be launching in a few minutes."

The Jewel of the Sea was not at all what they expected. It was nothing more than a pearl lugger, a

specialized boat used for harvesting oyster beds. It was not fancy, but it was certainly equipped to do the job.

Capt. Dave employed one deckhand and three divers for the trip. As the hired help pulled in the ropes and made ready to set off on the journey, Opal said to Carl, "Well, Hon, we have tried everything else. Who knows! This may be the day."

Hour after hour Carl and Opal sat in amazement as the divers would go down searching for precious pearls. They collected shells in a bag tied around their neck, and once filled, they sent the bag to the surface and waited for Capt. Dave or the deckhand to drop another bag down to them.

Capt. Dave explained that he didn't go for the new-fangled methods of pearl diving, including using scuba gear. "That kind of stuff is for sissies, and there ain't no sissies on this boat!"

The sun was setting. It was time to head back to the dock. Capt. Dave said, "All right, let's go back to the shop and see what we have."

After dumping all the oysters out on a big table the process of cracking them open began. Each time Capt. Dave or one of the hired help opened an oyster Carl and Opal's excitement level would rise. Time after time they came up empty.

As Capt. Dave opened the last oyster Carl and Opal felt an overwhelming sense of disappointment. For the first time all day, Capt. Dave did not have that carefree whimsical look on his face.

"I'm sorry we didn't find what you were looking for, Mate. Come back tomorrow and we will try it again. I have been doing this for many years, and I know some days are better than others. Are you game for another go at it tomorrow?"

"No thanks, I think we're going to go back to the hotel and reevaluate what we need to do next. I know you tried, and you don't have to give us our money back. Even though we didn't find what we were looking for, it was certainly a day to remember."

Opal nodded in agreement. "Capt. Dave, when Carl told me he met a real live pirate I didn't believe him. Whether it's an act for the tourist or not, you will always be a real live pirate to me."

Capt. Dave let out a big laugh and said, "Thank you, my dear. You will always be a real life adventure seeker to me. Before you go I just want to give you one piece of advice. Whatever you do, my lovely buckaroos, never settle for a substitute when looking for the real thing."

As the taxi was taking them back to the hotel, Carl and Opal had a very serious and subdued conversation.

"Honey, forgive me for giving you false hope. I just knew that we were close to finding *The Pearl of Great Price*. How could we miss? I felt everything was in our favor, including Capt. Dave. Most normal people would never go to the lengths we went to today. Think about it. What were the chances of me meeting this guy? If I had turned left yesterday morning when I took my walk instead of turning right…"

His voice trailed off. He didn't have the strength to say anymore. An overwhelming sense of failure filled their hearts.

There are times when a "sure thing" isn't so sure.

Carl and Opal headed for bed hoping that the next day would bring success.

# CHAPTER FIVE

# An Unsettled Desperation

She had been staring at the same spot on the beach for over an hour. The view from the villa was beyond description, but since arriving in Phuket the month before, Opal had felt a nagging sense of dread. It was nothing like the dream she had in Hyderabad or a premonition. It was just a sense that something was not right.

It started as soon as the plane took off from Broome International Airport. The original plan was to leave Broome and fly to French Polynesia. But, when Carl looked at a map again, there was something that drew his attention to Thailand. It didn't hurt that Phuket Island, Thailand, is affectionately referred to as the *Pearl of the Andaman* or *Pearl of the South*. As soon as they saw the word pearl they knew this was the place they needed to explore. Maybe, just maybe, this would be the place to find *The Pearl of Great Price*.

She brought up the sense of dread to Carl on more than one occasion. In the last conversation they had about it, Carl said maybe it was the memory of the tsunami that struck there in 2004 that made her feel that way.

"You know, Honey, a lot of people lost their lives that day. Maybe the whole area is depressed, and it's rubbing off on you."

Not wanting to be a problem or cause an argument Opal accepted his explanation. She didn't want to make a big deal about it. After all, who could be sad or depressed in a place like this? Opal didn't think the beauty of Western Australia could be matched, that is, until they landed in Thailand. Traveling to Phuket City was not easy but well worth it once they arrived. The locals were friendly and helpful. They seemed so determined to make their stay as pleasant as possible.

They decided to stay at a nice beach resort. They knew this resort was a melting pot for tourists from all over the world. From this location it was easy to get to shops and pearl farms located throughout the Island. It was nonstop shopping and looking. Unfortunately, they always came up empty. Would *The Pearl* ever be found?

One evening, after a long day of shopping they decided to not talk about pearls. They would just go out on the town and find a fancy restaurant. After their meal arrived, Opal noticed an exasperated look on Carl's face.

"What's the matter, Sweetheart? Are you beginning to feel the same sense of dread that I've been feeling, or are you just not hungry? You haven't touched a thing on your plate."

After a few more minutes of silence, Carl finally spoke up.

"I guess I'm not as hungry as I thought. Maybe I'm just tired of looking for something that I'm not sure we will ever find. I'm not ready to give up, but maybe what we need to do is take a break. If you think about it, since our journey began, we have taken very little time for ourselves. In Hyderabad it was the weird encounter with the man in the black Mercedes. In Broome we got our hopes up with Capt. Dave. You know, I think it's time for a little R&R. What do you think?"

Opal was surprised to hear what Carl was saying. She was tired too, and the feeling of dread would not seem to leave. But, she was not willing to give up on the search.

"Sweetheart, if that's what you think we need to do then I will certainly agree that a few days of R&R

might be just the ticket. Please promise me that we will continue the search and not give up."

Opal needed his reassurance, because she did not want to take a few days of rest and relaxation and suddenly give up and go home.

"Don't worry, hon, I'm not giving up. I just think it would be good to step away and clear our heads."

Opal agreed, and they both decided to start their break the next morning.

✠

Lying under a cabana on the beach the next day was a little slice of heaven. Sipping on a cold lemonade and watching seagulls dive for food made it all the more enjoyable.

Opal looked over at Carl and said, "This was a wonderful idea, Sweetheart. We both needed this."

"Thank you, Hon, I'm glad you agree. I feel better already."

Opal decided she could take the heat no longer. It was time for a swim. There was something about the sun and the sandy beach that seemed to wash away the sense of dread she had lived with for the past several weeks.

"Come on, Lazybones, get up and join me. I'll beat you to the water. Whoever jumps in first wins – loser buys dinner," yelled Opal.

Frankly, Carl was having too much fun lying on the chaise lounge sipping lemonade.

"Go ahead, sweetheart, jump in. I'll join you in a few minutes."

Opal walked out a ways into the ocean waves, dove under the water and started to swim. She thought, "This is incredible, I can't believe we waited this long to take some time to relax."

Paddling around in about 4 feet of water she felt like a little girl again.

Every once in a while she would let out a screech that would cause Carl to look over and give her a big smile.

"You're doing great, honey, just don't go out too far. If you see a shark remember to punch him in the nose and drag him up here. I'll cook him for supper," laughed Carl.

Suddenly, Opal felt the slightest brush along her calf. "I wonder what that was," she thought.

She knew the ocean was filled with a lot of strange and weird creatures, not to mention floating seaweed.

So she pushed it out of her mind and continued to splash around. Suddenly, without warning, she felt a rush of nausea followed by excruciating pain. She stood straight up holding her breath hoping it would go away. She realized it was time to make her way back to the beach. About 20 feet from the shore, Opal doubled over and fell face down in the surf. In her mind she was screaming, "What is happening to me? This can't be real!"

She kept thinking that Carl would see her, and come to her rescue. She finally was able to get enough strength to get up on all fours and scream…

"CARL… HELP ME… PLEASE HURRY!"

Not only did Carl hear her screams, but a lifeguard stationed close by also heard her call. The lifeguard and Carl reached Opal at the same time. Each taking an arm, they dragged Opal to the safety of the sand.

Turning her over, the lifeguard examined her to try to find the source of her pain. He noticed a small red streak on the back of her calf.

"Oh no, it looks like a Box Jellyfish sting. I've seen this before! We don't have much time. We have to get her medical help now!" yelled the lifeguard.

Carl was confused.

"I've always heard jellyfish stings were rather harmless. The pain usually goes away in just a few minutes. How could she be having such a serious reaction?"

The lifeguard was too busy dialing the emergency number to bother answering Carl's question.

Having been trained with enough medical knowledge to know the warning signs, the lifeguard checked her breathing. He noticed it was sporadic and very shallow.

"She's going into cardiac arrest; get out of the way!"

Immediately he began administering CPR. Carl, normally calm in stressful situations, could not contain his emotions. Watching someone give the love of his life CPR was more than he could handle.

"What's happening? Is she going to die? I don't understand. She was just swimming around." He screamed at the top of his lungs to the lifeguard. "DON'T YOU LET HER DIE!"

A few minutes later the emergency personnel arrived. As they loaded Opal on the stretcher into the back of the ambulance, Carl wheeled around and said to the lifeguard., "I don't know what we would've done if you had not been so close by. Thank you from the bottom of my heart. Please, tell me your name."

The young man simply smiled and said, "No thanks necessary. It's just part of my job. I know your wife is going to be all right. My name is Apson."

With that short answer the lifeguard turned and walked casually in the other direction, as if he already knew the outcome.

Carl held Opal's hand all the way to Phuket International Hospital. He was not sure if she could hear or understand what he was saying, but he continued to give her words of encouragement.

He leaned down and whispered in her ear, "You are not going anywhere without me. I refuse to let you! You hear me? You have to stay here!"

The trauma team had been alerted in advance. This was not the first time they had dealt with the deadly sting of the Box Jellyfish. As soon as the ambulance pulled up to the door they sprang into action.

Carl watched as they wheeled Opal back to the Trauma Center. He tried to accompany her, but the attending physician insisted, "No, stay in the waiting room area. I will come and talk to you as soon as I know something."

After an hour of waiting, Dr. Chusak sat down with Carl to explain Opal's condition.

"Sir, your wife is going to be just fine. It was a close call. It was fortunate the lifeguard knew exactly what to do. We have seen cases where proper medical attention to this type of deadly sting was not given. Without proper treatment it is possible for the patient to die. You see, your wife was stung by one of the deadliest creatures in the world. We have administered the proper antidote to the venom, and I believe within two or three weeks she will be as good as new. She will need lots of rest and encouragement. She has been through a very difficult ordeal."

Later that evening Opal was moved to the intensive care unit on the fifth floor. Although most visitors were only allowed 10 minutes with the patient, as her husband, Carl was allowed to stay with her full-time. Around 10 o'clock that night, to Carl's utter joy, Opal opened her eyes.

"Welcome back, honey. You can't believe how wonderful it is to see your beautiful blue eyes."

Opal, though weak, wanted to know all the details. The last thing she remembered was the excruciating pain and falling into the surf. Everything after that was a blank.

"Honey, the doctor says you're going to be just fine. It is going to take a few weeks of rest and recuperation with lots of love and encouragement from me, but he says you're going to be good as new."

He kept trying to tell her more, but it was hard because, he could not hold back the tears.

"Oh, Sweetheart, I don't think I've ever felt such fear and desperation in my life. Watching you in so much pain hurt me in places that I never thought I could hurt. I wanted to swap places with you and take the pain, but I couldn't."

Gently squeezing her hand he said, "I don't think I could go on without you, and to think in a split second I almost lost you."

She didn't have the strength to reply; only giving him a squeeze of the hand and a flicker of a smile. Once Carl saw her smile he knew everything was going to be okay.

After a few more days in the hospital, the doctors allowed Carl to take her back to the villa to continue her recuperation. Late one afternoon, while Opal was resting, Carl decided to thank the lifeguard who was mainly responsible for saving her life. He headed down the familiar trail to the beach and to the general area where he almost lost her. After a short walk, he found himself standing in front of the lifeguard station.

Carl spoke to the lifeguard on duty.

"Excuse me sir, I'm looking for a young man named Apson. He was on duty the day my wife was stung by a Box Jellyfish. Had it not been for him, I don't think she would be with us today. Can you help me?"

"Sorry, sir, but there isn't a lifeguard by that name who works this portion of the beach. Maybe you are in the wrong place."

Carl asked the lifeguard to come down and talk to him a minute, because he wanted to explain again why he was looking for the lifeguard.

"I know I am in the right place, and I remember his name, so please help me. I want to thank him."

After listening to a few more minutes of the story the lifeguard finally said, "Sir, I have been working this beach for over five years, and there has never been a lifeguard by that name. I know you want to thank him, but I can't help you."

Carl walked up and down the beach for over two hours asking if anyone had heard or knew of a lifeguard named Apson. The answer was always the same, "No."

It's as if the young man never existed. Carl decided to let it go and just be thankful that whoever he was, he was in the right place at the right time.

Sometimes, life doesn't give you the answers you're

looking for. By now Carl was beginning to get used to things that couldn't be explained.

✠

One of Carl's favorite activities since arriving in Phuket was to take late-night walks on the beach. He chose to forego the walks while Opal recovered. He did not want to leave her alone. One evening, since she seemed to be getting stronger, he thought it would be all right to leave her alone for a short period of time. He needed some time to think.

As Carl strolled along the beach he got lost in his thoughts and walked further than he intended. He looked at his watch and noticed he been gone for over an hour. It was time to get back to the villa.

When Carl walked into the bedroom he found Opal propped up watching television. "Honey, sorry it took so long, I just needed some time to think. Do you need anything?"

"No, Sweetheart, I'm fine. Is everything all right?"

Carl decided it was time to tell her what was really on his mind.

"I've been thinking about something, and I want to be honest with you. I think it's time to go home."

Opal turned off the television and looked straight at him.

"But, you said after our R&R we would continue to search for *The Pearl*? I don't understand. Why all of a sudden do you want to go home?"

Carl sat down on the bed.

"Honey, I almost lost you. I didn't know how much I loved you until I saw you lying on the beach fighting for your life. Something happened on the inside of me, and it's hard to explain. All I know is that I could not dream of going on without you. I have decided that maybe you are my pearl, and there's nothing in this world that could pull me away from you. I could never give you up under any circumstance!"

Opal really didn't know how to respond except to say, "Oh Carl, I love you too, and you are my very breath. You are my pearl as well, but I think there is more to it than what we know. I will follow your lead, but please sleep on it tonight before you make the final decision."

After getting ready for bed, Carl leaned over to give her a good night kiss.

"I will sleep on it, and we can talk more about it in the morning, but right now my mind is made up. It's time to go home."

Opal was too tired to engage in any more conversation and drifted off to sleep knowing that Carl would make the right decision.

They were both up early the next morning. Opal decided to wait and let Carl bring up the subject.

"Hon, I have made a decision. I hope you are willing to go along with it."

Opal held her breath, waiting to hear his decision.

"Do you remember before we came here we were going to go to Tahiti? Well, I think instead of going home we need to head in that direction. What do you think?"

Opal was overjoyed. In her heart of hearts she knew their journey was not over. She just needed to give him a little time to sort things out. After all, their stay in Phuket was a little more than they bargained for.

"Like I said last night, I will follow your lead. You and I started this journey together, and we are going to finish it together. *The Pearl* is out there somewhere. Who knows, maybe we will find it in Tahiti."

A few days later, as the driver was loading their luggage to take them to the airport, Opal said, "We are very early for our flight. Why don't you run down to the beach and thank that nice young lifeguard who saved my life? I'll just wait for you in the van."

Carl just looked at her and smiled, "Let's go on to the airport, and I'll explain what I've learned about the lifeguard on the way to the airport. You're not going to believe it."

Unexplained things, and going home was becoming a constant theme. Unwanted distractions have a way of doing that at times.

# CHAPTER SIX

# An Echo from
# the Past

One of the first things you learn when traveling is to check the local weather before you arrive. Seemed Carl forgot that little detail! Arriving in January is not the best time of year to be spending time in Tahiti. It's called the rainy season for a reason!

Before venturing out to the other islands that collectively make up French Polynesia, Carl and Opal decided to make Papeete home base.

"How many days has it been raining?" asked Carl.

Opal quipped, "I don't know, 12 or 13; I've lost count. Do you think it'll ever stop?"

"Your guess is as good as mine. Don't remind me

again that I didn't look at the weather before coming here. Just let it go."

The hotel was beautiful, but as each day passed by it seemed more like a prison than a seaside slice of heaven. There is such a thing as too much togetherness!

Carl decided it was time to lighten the mood. "Just think, Hon, that little grain of sand rubbing the oyster the wrong way can make a beautiful pearl."

Opal never batted an eye or cracked a smile. "If that's the case, if you keep it up, you better find a wheelbarrow, because there's going to be a 200 pound pearl produced in this room!"

Carl didn't bother to ask for an interpretation. So much for lighthearted humor on a rainy afternoon!

Occasionally they would try to visit shops in the area, but the rainy weather seemed to sap their strength. They had high hopes *The Pearl* would be found in the *Land of Black Pearls*. So far, they were batting zero.

After about a month of each day looking like the day before, they decided to relax and not worry about trying to find *The Pearl* until the rain let up.

"You hungry?"

"I could eat. What did you have in mind?"

"It's totally up to you, sweetheart. What are you in the mood for?"

Opal was not known for making fast culinary decisions. "Oh, I don't care, you name it. I'll go wherever you want to go."

"Okay, then, how about some good old-fashioned American food at that little diner we saw yesterday?"

"Try something else; that place didn't look very clean."

"How about that beautiful French restaurant we saw downtown?"

"Nope, try again."

"Okay, Hon, you pick it."

"No, that's all right, you decide. I'll go wherever you want to go."

Carl didn't bother to try to figure it out. He just said, "Come on, let's get a taxi, and I'll surprise you."

He had read about the Le Royal Restaurant in a brochure provided by the hotel staff. He'd been waiting for a chance to go there, and since Opal didn't have a particular food in mind, he thought this would be a good chance to check it out.

As they drove up to the front of the restaurant the taxi driver said, "You have made a good choice, if you don't mind me saying. The tourists have not found this place yet, but you can be sure that the locals know all about it. Not only is the food great, but each evening a local band provides entertainment."

"So far, so good," Carl mused.

The tension and the stress seemed to lift as they enjoyed a sumptuous meal. Carl and Opal were getting back to their old selves.

✠

"Look over there, Honey. You see the man standing by the bar? Who does he look like?"

"You mean the big guy with gray hair and a beard?"

"Yeah, that's the one. If I didn't know better I would say that Big Jim Griffin has a twin brother."

Opal continued staring.

"You mean the guy who used to go with you on buying trips? I thought he died several years ago."

"No, that wasn't the guy I told you about who died. Big Jim was very much alive the last time I saw him. Well, anyway, that can't be him. It's not possible.

Now they were both staring at the man and totally forgot about their dessert.

"Oh, Lord, he's walking this way. Should I say something?" whispered Carl.

Before she had a chance to respond, the big guy stood in front of their table and let out a huge roar – "YOU HAVE GOT TO BE KIDDING ME! CARL, IS THAT YOU? WHAT IN THE WORLD ARE YOU DOING HERE?"

Carl jumped up and grabbed his old friend.

"What am I doing here? What are you doing here? Come here, big guy, and give me a hug. You remember Opal, don't you?"

"Oh yes, of course I do. How are you young lady? It's good to see you're still around to keep this guy straight," laughed Big Jim.

After a few minutes of catching up, Big Jim offered a suggestion, "Why don't we go back to my place? It's only a few miles from here, and we can talk without all this noise."

They both nodded in agreement.

"I must admit, Big Jim, this is one of the most beautiful homes I have ever seen. I knew you did well in the jewelry business, but I had no idea you did this well," smiled Carl.

"Let's just say I did well, and obviously you did, too. You don't come to Tahiti on a small budget. Let's face it, the jewelry business was good for both of us."

Carl and Opal both agreed. The next hour or so Carl and Big Jim reminisced about old times. They remembered him as a lovable, carefree teddy bear, but tonight he had a different edge about him.

It had been years since they saw him last, and people do change.

Occasionally, they would stop talking and look at each other and say, "Can you believe that we are sitting here. What are the chances of that happening?"

Opal interrupted the trip down memory lane. She had a few questions of her own.

"So, where is Olivia? Is she visiting friends or family back in the states?

The last time Opal remembered seeing Big Jim was at a retirement dinner for one of their mutual friends that worked at the railroad. Olivia was seated next to her at the table and couldn't stop talking about how wonderful Big Jim was.

"No, she's not traveling."

Opal decided to push the envelope. "Well, where is she? I would love to catch up with her?"

The mood in the room suddenly shifted.

"Like I said, she is not traveling, and she's not here. So, let's just drop it, okay?

Opal made a fundamental mistake of assumption. "So, how long have you two been divorced? I know it's a touchy subject, and forgive me for prying, but I remember you two were so happy together. What happened?"

Things quickly started to go downhill.

"If you must know, we are not divorced at all. Olivia and I were married for 42 years. She was my high school sweetheart, the love of my life. As a matter of fact, you are sitting in her dream home."

"Please forgive me, obviously I have touched a nerve. I didn't mean to spoil the happy mood."

Carl chimed in. "If you don't feel like talking about it, we understand. Maybe it's best if Opal and I call a taxi and head back to the hotel. It's getting late."

"No, no, it's okay. I might as well tell you the whole story. About six years ago Olivia was having some health issues and went for a checkup. I will never forget the day the doctor came in and said there was a spot on her right lung. They did a biopsy, and it wasn't good.

When they told us it was cancer we were in a state of shock. She never smoked, always watched her diet, and yet they said it was progressing rapidly and treatment had to start immediately.

After surgery and rounds of chemotherapy and radiation, it looked like we were out of the woods. It was a struggle, but slowly things were getting back to normal.

It was right after her last checkup that we decided it was time to fulfill our dream. We had vacationed here in Tahiti many years ago and decided if there was one place on earth we could live out the rest of our lives together it would be here. It took two years to build the house. I didn't know two people could be so happy. We were like teenagers.

But, after a while, she started showing signs that something was not right. I won't bore you with the rest of the details. I lost the love of my life two years ago this April. Little did I know the rest of our lives would only last a few years."

Carl and Opal got up and sat next to Big Jim on the sofa. They put their arms around him and sat in silence.

Finally, Carl said, "I am so sorry. I had no idea you had been through such a horrific ordeal."

Carl refused to let his mind take him back to the

beach in Phuket where he almost lost the love of his life. It was not time for that.

Wiping his eyes, Big Jim said, "Let's change the subject. How did you end up in Tahiti? Vacation, business, or what?"

Carl started at the beginning. For the next two hours he told him everything, including the strange meeting with the Jamaican in Ocho Rios. He tried to choose his words carefully. Not everyone would understand embarking on a journey to places they had never been to find something they had never seen.

Carl stopped talking, took a deep breath and said, "Why don't we finish the rest of this another time? It's getting late."

"You're right," smiled Big Jim, "it is getting late and it's way past my bedtime. If you would like, I will call your hotel tomorrow, say around 2 o'clock, and we can set up a late lunch. I definitely want to hear the rest of the story."

The phone rang at 2 o'clock sharp the next afternoon.

"What did he say?"

"He wants to meet us at the InterContinental Resort. He said it was a beautiful place with an outdoor restaurant right on the beach. I told him we will meet him there."

Big Jim was already there when they arrived. He waved them over to the table, gave them a hug and said, "Let's eat. I'm starving!"

Big Jim pushed back from the table.

"Last night you left me in Western Australia. So, you gonna finish the story or what?"

Carl thought he might as well jump in and tell him everything.

"Listen, I am about to bring you up-to-date, but I want you to know before I tell you about what happened in Phuket that I am in no way comparing it to what you have been through."

Carl finished telling him about almost losing Opal on the beach. He didn't leave out any details.

"So, is that it?"

"Yep, pretty much. After that we decided to leave and come to Tahiti."

Carl was getting a different vibe from Big Jim than what he expected. He was hoping after telling the story that Big Jim would offer to assist them in finding *The Pearl of Great Price*.

"Let me get this straight. You and Opal decided to leave your home, kids and grandkids and travel halfway around the world to find this so-called *Pearl of Great Price*? And, you did all this based on a crumpled up note handed to you by some strange Jamaican dude years ago? Does that about sum it up?"

"Well, if you put it that way, I guess so."

A dark cloud just rolled in and started to rain on Carl and Opal's parade.

"Let me tell you something, Carl. You and Opal have no idea the pain I have been through. I lost my pearl of great price, and her name was Olivia. You talk about traveling halfway around the world, spending all of this money, just to find some silly Pearl. You don't even realize that you have it sitting beside you!"

"Hang on, Big Jim. I didn't mean to upset you. You asked me to tell you how we ended up in Tahiti. This was not a journey that we decided to take on a whim. It was well thought out, planned, and up until this point, exciting. Yes, I know we had the Phuket incident, but all in all, it's been wonderful."

At this point Big Jim was almost shouting.

"You two are on a fool's journey, pure and simple! There is no such thing as a *Pearl of Great Price*! You have been hoodwinked, bamboozled, duped, and it's time to grow up and go home!"

Dumbfounded at this outburst, Carl and Opal just looked at each other.

"Wow! Tell us how you really feel," laughed Opal, trying to lighten the mood.

Big Jim didn't laugh. He lit in again, "All I'm saying is that my life was perfect in every way. We had our dream home, more money than we needed to live, and most of all each other. My whole life was wrapped up in her, and now I have nothing, because I don't have her."

Carl tried to say something, but Big Jim kept going.

"I just don't understand. I think you're on a fool's mission."

Carl had to respond.

"I can't explain it. All I know is this is something we have to do. I don't expect you to understand it."

"You're right; I don't!"

"Listen," Carl reasoned, "all of us have had difficulties, trials and heartaches. You're not the only one. You can choose. You can either get bitter or get better. The choice is up to you."

Big Jim had heard enough.

Suddenly, while Carl was still trying to explain, Big Jim got up and walked toward the waitress. He grabbed the check out of her hand and kept walking. Before he got to the door he stopped, turned around and said, "Hope you find what you're looking for, but if you want my advice... DON'T BE A FOOL! GO HOME!"

And he was gone.

Carl and Opal didn't say two words the rest of the day. They were in a state of shock. They were subdued and saddened as they reflected on their short reunion with their old friend, Jim.

Finally, Opal broke the silence.

"Well, that was something."

"Yep, that was something, all right. I thought maybe running into Big Jim was some kind of divine coincidence. I kept thinking he might hear our story and help us. You just never know how people change."

"Boy, were you wrong."

"How was I supposed to know? I haven't seen him in years and had no idea that he moved here. And, had no idea that Olivia had died, so don't blame me."

"I'm not blaming you, Sweetheart. Do you think he was right? Should we forget about trying to find the elusive *Pearl of Great Price*?"

"Seems like every time I turn around we are having this conversation about going home. Last time it was my turn. Now, it's your turn. Is that what you want to do?"

"Do you want me to be honest with you?" said Opal.

"Are you telling me you haven't been?"

"No, of course not. I've always tried to be open and honest with you. Here's my thought – we started this journey together to find something missing in our lives. That hunger has not left. I don't care what Big Jim said. All I know is, we shouldn't stop until we give it our best effort."

"You know what I say to that?"

"What?"

"I agree one hundred percent. Let's make an agreement right now. No more talk of going home until we find what we're looking for. Agreed?"

"Absolutely, I agree!"

"Tomorrow is a brand-new day. Now, let's get some sleep."

The rain had finally let up, and they continued their search. Over the next three weeks they visited many places on the island looking for the elusive *Pearl*. Each time they were handed a tray of pearls they knew this could be the day they found it. Unfortunately, it never happened.

Occasionally, Big Jim would come up in a conversation.

"I know you were disappointed that he was not the same lovable, carefree guy you once knew years ago," said Opal. "It didn't take much of our story for his bitterness to show, did it?"

"Unfortunately not," lamented Carl. "It was obvious he is still in a lot of pain. Life can bring such pain."

"Honey, getting counsel from a good friend is a good thing. But, just because a person is a good friend does not mean his or her advice is always good. Don't let what he said at the restaurant bother you anymore."

Opal assured Carl she understood why Big Jim was so negative, and that she wasn't going to let it bother her any longer.

"I got his address. Let's keep in touch with him."

"Let's do."

They both agreed Tahiti was a beautiful place to visit, but it was time to move on.

"Honey, you ready to keep moving?"

"Sure, where to?

"I'm not sure, yet. Let's sleep on it and talk about it after breakfast."

"As long as it doesn't involve strange men in black Mercedes, a wanna be pirate, Box Jellyfish or old friends from the past, I'm game!"

"Good to see you haven't lost your sense of humor," laughed Carl.

"Nope, sometimes you have to laugh to keep from crying."

Opal went on, "I guess sometimes you have to discover through personal loss that you can't hold on too tightly to the things of this life. I hope Big Jim will be all right."

# CHAPTER SEVEN

## An Illusion
in Life

Before they left Tahiti, they decided it was time to check in with the kids. Hearing familiar voices from home can be a good thing or a bad thing. It's always good to talk to loved ones because you miss them so much. But, it can also stir up a higher level of homesickness.

"Goodbye, Honey, it was great hearing your voice. I am glad everything is good on the home front. Give my love to the grandkids. Tell them that Pawpaw and Mimi will be home soon bringing lots of surprises."

Carl handed the phone to Opal.

He walked out on the patio to enjoy an ice-cold

lemonade while Opal continued to talk to their oldest daughter.

A little later Opal took the lemonade out of Carl's hand and began to sip.

He said, "Are you okay?"

"Yes, I'm fine. Sometimes I think it's better not to call. You know the old saying, 'no news is good news'? Maybe we need to think about using that as a rule of thumb before calling again."

There was something their oldest daughter said to Opal that she did not want to bring up quite yet. She needed some time to think more about their conversation.

✠

"Are you ready to tell me what's bothering you? You haven't been the same since you got off the phone."

Opal decided she might as well tell Carl about the conversation. She didn't know how to frame the words exactly but gave it a shot.

"The conversation was fine. Everybody is doing well: no problems and no crisis. But, near the end of the conversation, Gretchen asked me a question."

"Let me guess... When are we coming home?"

"Nope, not even close. As a matter of fact, our coming home was not even mentioned."

They always considered their oldest child as the mother hen of the children. She never said much but was always concerned about everyone, especially her mom and dad.

"Enough with the suspense. What did the wise one ask you?"

"She wanted to know if we had thought about the idea that *The Pearl of Great Price* might not be a literal pearl. That maybe that's why we haven't been able to find it."

Carl paused before answering. He didn't want to say something he might regret.

Calmly, he said, "So, what did you say?"

"I reminded her about the note we received in Jamaica. I told her that we were sure that our search was for the *Perfect Pearl*. And no, we haven't considered any other possibilities."

"Sounds like a perfectly reasonable answer. So, why are you still bothered?"

"Can we just talk about this some other time? I just need a mental break not a mental break down. And, by the way, it might be a good idea to figure out where we're going next."

Opal felt that it was better to end the conversation now than tell him she felt that maybe their daughter was right. Maybe it was time to consider that *The Pearl of Great Price* as a symbol of something else that was missing in their lives. What that something was she didn't know, but at least she was willing to consider other options.

The next morning after breakfast Carl pulled out a notebook and a map.

"I've decided to be open-minded about this. I'm willing to concede that maybe our daughter was right. I guess anything is possible. Maybe we need to consider *The Pearl* is not literal, but symbolic. I hate to think that we've been looking for the wrong thing this whole time."

"Sweetheart, I am so relieved. I've been thinking the same thing. So what do we do now?"

Carl spread the map out on the table.

"You see these three circles?"

Opal leaned over and saw that he had circled Rome, Paris and New York.

"Okay, I give up. What does that mean?"

"It means, pack your bags. It's time to hit the road. I've decided those three cities represent *intellectualism, culture, and money*. If there's something we're missing, maybe we will find it in one of those places."

As they were carrying their luggage through the lobby to catch the shuttle, Carl walked right by a plaque hanging on the wall.

It read –

*"Life is full of mystery, almost like a shell game. Now you see it, now you don't. But in your heart of hearts somehow you always know the real thing. So, settling for less than the genuine should never be an option."*

Too bad he didn't stop long enough to consider the meaning.

Carl and Opal were about to fall for one of the oldest tricks in the book: An Illusion is nothing more than having a fantastic plan or desire that causes an erroneous belief or perception.

# CHAPTER EIGHT

# An Empty Trip Home

Carl picked up his briefcase and put his arm around Opal. "Come on, sweetheart, they called our flight number. It's time to leave."

Settling into their seats, they thought this would be a good time to review their recent experiences, especially the exciting trips they had made to Rome, Paris and New York. They were in agreement that *The Pearl of Great Price,* although elusive, would not be found by just adding more education, money or religion to their lives. Every place they visited was awe-inspiring, to say the least. But, the inspiration they felt was no substitute for the hunger in their hearts.

Opal leaned over, put her head on his shoulder and said, "Thank you for taking me on such a wonderful adventure. Maybe taking the trips to Rome, Paris and New York was a bit of a stretch. I was hoping it would be the answer."

"It was a long shot, but at least we tried. If we had not made the effort, we would always wonder if we gave it 100%."

As quickly as they left for their final adventure, it was over. The excitement they felt at the beginning of the three-city search did not compare to the disappointment they felt going home. Of course, they wanted to see their children and grandchildren, but the hunger in their hearts had only increased over time. Their dream had turned into a nightmare.

The last email they sent to the children from New York summed it up:

"We're coming home – all has failed."

✠

They were all waiting. A huge crowd of family, friends, and even casual acquaintances were standing on tiptoes waiting for Carl and Opal to deplane. Word had spread throughout the community that this respected couple was returning from the adventure of a lifetime.

It was not surprising so many people showed up to welcome them home.

The crowd waited with anticipation. Suddenly they saw them. The look on Carl and Opal's face was not what everyone had expected. It was a look of disappointment and embarrassment. After a quick greeting and hugs all around, they hurriedly headed to collect their bags. It was as if no one knew what to say. They wanted to ask questions about the trip, but this just didn't seem the right time or place. With such a thick fog of disappointment hanging in the air the children decided not to press the issue. There would be time to talk later.

After one of the longest rides home in the history of rides home, they drove up to the old home place. It had been perfectly maintained by the children while they were away. It is said that home is where the heart is, and today their heart was certainly in their home. They knew their home would offer a refuge, a safe haven of rest, but they knew at some point they would have to explain to their family why they failed.

Carl and Opal dropped their luggage in the living room and just held on to each other.

With tears streaming down his face, Carl asked, "Sweetheart, can you ever forgive me?"

"Forgive you for what?"

"I failed you in so many ways. I took you around the world looking for something to fill the emptiness in our hearts. And as we stand here together, the emptiness is still there."

Opal cupped his face in her hands.

"You haven't failed me any more than I have failed you! It's obvious that life has failed us both. We have followed our hearts to try to find *The Pearl of Great Price*. We were willing to do whatever it took to find it."

Carl wiped away tears as Opal continued.

"Think about it. We have both worked hard, raised great children and have many wonderful friends. When that didn't satisfy us completely we were willing to spend thousands of dollars and travel all over the world to search for an answer. And, what did it bring?"

She answered her own question:

"Zero…nothing! We are back to where we started: emptier than before we left. So, you see sweetheart, it's not your fault – there is simply NO PEARL to be found!"

All they wanted to do now was crawl under the covers and hide from the rest of the world. They knew they were going to face their children later with a somewhat reasonable explanation. Holding each other more tenderly than they ever had before, they fell off to sleep hoping against hope that tomorrow would be better.

In spite of their disappointment, they both agreed it was good to be eating breakfast at their own table for a change.

No sooner had they sat down to eat when the phone rang. Their oldest daughter decided it would be a good idea to check on them.

"Are you okay?"

"We are fine, sweetheart, and thank you for asking. We got a little sleep, and I have to admit it felt good being back in our own bed again."

The real purpose of the phone call was to make plans for a family meal that evening. Everyone wanted to know about their long mysterious trip. As the day progressed, Carl and Opal slowly settled in and decided that evening they would tell the whole story.

It has been said the death of a dream is almost like the slow agonizing death of a loved one. There is a certain sense of relief when you realize it's finally over. It takes a miracle to resurrect dead dreams, and a miracle would surely be needed for this one.

The feeling of dread left them as they anticipated a happy reunion with their children and grandchildren. As everyone gathered for the meal, everyone felt a relief for it seemed that Mom and Dad were okay. Based on what they had witnessed at the airport, no one was sure what they were going to encounter that evening. But, much to everyone's joy, the evening seemed like old times: catching up with family happenings, making fun of dad at the dinner table, and a whole lot of love passed around made the night all the more enjoyable.

Carl and Opal knew at some point the question would be asked. Finally, their oldest son, Paul who always had such a tender heart, popped the question everyone wanted to know, "So, Mom and Dad, are you ready to tell us about your trip?"

Carl and Opal both felt safe and secure enough to tell them about their adventure. For over two hours everyone sat spellbound as they shared in detail about all the wonderful places they had visited and the experiences they had shared.

They didn't leave anything out. They recounted the strange encounter with a man in the black Mercedes in Hyderabad. Everyone erupted in laughter as they heard about Capt. Dave, the wannabe pirate in Broome, Australia. Carl and Opal were particularly careful about sharing the details of almost losing Mom on the beach in Phuket, Thailand. But, he had to tell them about trying to find the lifeguard who saved Opal's life who was nowhere to be found. They all agreed the trip was full of strange and unusual occurrences.

Opal interrupted Carl, "Honey, let me tell them about running into Big Jim in Tahiti."

For the next 30 minutes Opal related the strange experience of meeting an old friend in such a faraway place. She told them about Big Jim's bitterness over losing his wife Olivia and how he tried to talk them out of continuing on with such a losing proposition.

"We decided then and there it was good to see an old friend, but we were not going to let him talk us out of our goal to find *The Pearl of Great Price*."

Carl took Opal by the hand and looked at the group.

"Many times during our search we believed we were close to finding *The Pearl*. We looked at what seemed to be thousands of pearls, and none of them were perfect or priceless. None of them gave any hint of filling the empty hole in our hearts. Each time we landed in a new city we would get our hopes up that maybe this would be the place. Obviously, we were wrong."

Carl realized the night was getting away from them and decided to wrap it up.

"Let me finish by saying we thought maybe we had missed it, and *The Pearl* was not literal but symbolic of something we were missing. You see, that's why we spent time in Rome, Paris and New York. Maybe I'll go into the details of that at a later time, but for now let me just say the search for *The Pearl* has ended. We gave it our best effort, and it's time to get on with the rest of our lives."

When the night was finally over, no one wanted to leave. It was one of those nights when everything seemed perfect, except for the obvious disappointment of Mom and Dad. Everyone was relieved they were home safe and sound and felt that everything was going to be all right.

Their oldest daughter was the last to leave, and she summed it up for the rest of the family.

"We are so happy to have you back. I know this was something you had to do. Let's face it. You had to get this out of your system. Now that you have, I'm sure everything will return to normal. After all, it's family and friends that matter the most."

Carl and Opal stood on the front porch and waved as everyone pulled away. He turned to Opal and said, "Was she right? Is that really all that matters?"

"Maybe so, maybe not. That's a conversation we will

have to have another time. Let's go to bed now. I am worn out."

Carl knew enough not to push her to talk more that evening. In spite of being home with family and friends, the emptiness in his heart would not go away. He could never forget the note he was handed in Ocho Rios, but he reminded himself... it was over.

✠

Carl had no idea how easy it was to slip back into the old routine. From that night on life, took on the same shade of gray. There was no more talk of searching for the elusive *Pearl*. Previously, he may have thought he would never give up the search, but life has a way of numbing you to your dreams.

Family and friends once again found themselves at the top of the priority list. Days were filled with school activities with the grandchildren, and at least three nights a week, evenings out with old friends catching up on all they had missed while they were gone.

The Christmas holidays came and went with another familiar New Year's Eve celebration. Yes, life had returned to normal. Everything was back to 'business as usual' with only an occasional fleeting thought of their emptiness.

As spring approached, they were about to get one of the biggest surprises of their life. Unknown to them, their children were planning a 50th wedding anniversary celebration in their honor. This was a covert operation the CIA would have been proud of. Nothing would be left out – after all, not many couples make it to a half a century!

The children were hoping this would be an evening to remember, especially in light of their Mom and Dad's failure to find their *Pearl*. The party might not fill the void completely, but in their mind, at least it was a start.

On the night of April 28, *Operation Golden Surprise* was launched. They convinced Carl and Opal that a small dinner party just for the family was going to be held at a local restaurant. At 6:30 sharp the longest limousine they had ever seen pulled up to their front door. Like two teenagers going to the prom, they eagerly headed toward the limousine. The chauffeur walked ahead of them and was just about to open the door for Opal, but Carl stepped in front of him and said, "Excuse me, sir, I appreciate the gesture, but fifty years ago today I opened the door for the first time for my beautiful new bride, and I want you to know she's more beautiful today than she was then; so please allow me."

Carl leaned forward in the seat and looked out the window.

"Driver, I'm not sure, but I don't think this is the way to the restaurant."

"I don't know about that. I'm just following the directions that were given to me."

The happy couple really didn't care. After all, it's not every day you ride in the back of a limo listening to soft romantic music, just enjoying one another's company.

The limo turned left on Main Street and immediately Carl recognized they were headed downtown. They stopped in front of the Opera House. It was easy to recognize what was going on, because the Marquis was lit up with.

## CARL AND OPAL
## CONGRATULATIONS ON YOUR 50TH

Over 300 friends and family gathered to honor them. As soon as they stepped onto the red carpet leading them to the top of the stairs to the ballroom, loud cheering could be heard two blocks away. Looking down from the top of the stairs was their family smiling from ear to ear, in obvious delight; they had pulled off the surprise of the century.

What a perfect night. A band played music from the Big Band Era. They took trips down memory lane with old friends. They enjoyed a night that would be burned into their memory for the rest of their lives.

The 50th anniversary cake was rolled to the platform. Their second son, Thom, served as master of ceremonies. He is Mr. Personality and a natural in front of a crowd. He took the microphone and began.

"Mom and Dad, before we cut the cake, a few of your friends would like to say something."

A few friends were an understatement. After an hour of listening to words of appreciation and love, the toasts had to be stopped or the cake was going to melt right before their eyes.

Their son took the microphone again.

"I know we are anxious to cut the cake and hear a word from Mom and Dad, but my brother and sister have something they would like to say. I told them to be brief, but I have to say, it's never worked before."

The room erupted in laughter. Each of the children took a turn at the microphone starting with the youngest.

Finally, the oldest daughter closed out. "Mom and Dad, you raised all of us to follow our dreams and believe that we could do anything we set our minds to. You taught us values about life that are still with us today.

When we did something wrong, you lovingly corrected us, and when we did something right, you were our biggest cheerleaders. We didn't choose you as our parents... we didn't have a say in the matter. But, I want you to know, if the choice had been left up to us, we would've chosen you every day of the week and twice on Sunday!"

Her voice became a little more serious.

"We all know how disappointed you were when you returned from your trip around the world looking for your *Pearl*. You have been so generous in helping others reach their goals and fulfill their dreams. We don't want to bring up a painful subject on such a happy occasion, but we just want to say that maybe somehow, someway, this celebration can ease the pain of not finding what you were looking for. We will always love you. You have never been a disappointment to us!"

By this time, everyone was standing, applauding and shouting 'speech, speech'.

Carl and Opal stood to their feet to address the crowd.

"We can never thank you enough for honoring us with this special evening. How could we ever repay our children for the anniversary of a lifetime? Words are inadequate and empty compared to what our hearts feel."

Carl pulled Opal closer to him.

"We have no regrets for trying to find the *Priceless Pearl*. The only regret we have is what seemed to be the wasted years not spent with our children and grandchildren. But, all that is over and behind us. We both agree; it's too late for us."

His words trailed off and faded into silence. He laid the microphone down on the podium.

Carl backed away from the podium ready to sit down. Opal abruptly picked up the microphone.

"I want everyone to know, we have each other, and our family; And, all of you, our dear friends – AND THAT'S ENOUGH!"

Another standing ovation followed her declaration.

It had long been announced that no gifts were allowed at the celebration, because a special collection had been taken for a very special gift.

Suddenly, the band struck up a loud fanfare as if to announce someone special. But, it wasn't someone, it was something. It was time to present a very special 50th anniversary gift from family and friends.

An old friend stepped to the microphone after the drumroll faded away. He was not just any friend; he was Carl's best man at their wedding some 50 years before.

He turned toward the precious couple.

"We wanted to give you a special gift that you would never forget, so we all chipped in and bought you a first-class trip to where it all began 50 years ago. We're sending you to the beaches of Ocho Rios, Jamaica for 10 days. You will be staying in the same beach side villa that you stayed in on your honeymoon. It's undergone a little renovation over the last 50 years, but believe me, you will recognize it for sure."

The atmosphere and emotion in the room was electric. Everyone, including Carl and Opal, was either shouting or weeping. It was a night of nights, just what the doctor ordered to ease the pain of disappointment.

As the limo pulled away from the curb, they could only wave to those standing around and shake their heads in disbelief.

After a night like that, sleep was hard to come by. As the sun was rising, Carl asked, "Are you awake?"

"Yes, of course, who could sleep after a night like that? Let me ask you something. Was it a dream or did the kids say something about Ocho Rios and a second honeymoon?"

"Honey, either we had the same dream, or you heard it right. Yes, they gave us a second honeymoon!"

"I'll make us some coffee, while you look for the envelope."

They both jumped out of bed at the same time. Carl remembered putting the envelope in the inside pocket of his tuxedo.

He emptied the contents of the envelope on the table. "Honey, look at this. Everything is included. First-class all the way."

As they scanned through the contents, they realized that the departure was only a week away. One thing they learned on their previous adventure was the fine art of travel.

"OK, Hon, it's time to get serious about packing. We have a lot to do in a short period of time."

To that they both agreed. The next few days passed quickly as they made the rounds to as many family and friends as possible thanking them for the marvelous celebration and unexpected gift.

Life has a way of coming full circle. It has been said "life is nothing more than a succession of lessons that must be lived to be understood." Carl and Opal were about to find out that resurrected dreams are more precious than gold.

# CHAPTER NINE

# An Unexpected Discovery

Arriving in Ocho Rios was like a dream come true. If there was one place they thought they would never visit again it would be the very resort where it all began 50 years before. The old saying, "The more things change, the more they stay the same," would certainly apply in this case. What was once a small villa on the beach had been transformed into a large, all-inclusive resort. It did not matter to Carl and Opal what changes and renovations had taken place over the years; the only thing that mattered was they were back to enjoy something that many couples do not experience – a second honeymoon after 50 years.

The first three days were a whirlwind of activity. Trying to find places they had visited before was a challenge. They did find a few gift shops and restaurants that looked familiar, but for the most part it was all new and much different than what they remembered from before. It really didn't matter, because they wanted to soak it all in and just enjoy each other's company.

One of their favorite things to do was to get up early and enjoy breakfast on the veranda overlooking the ocean. It was the morning of the fourth day when things started to change. After enjoying a delicious breakfast, old feelings were about to come to the surface. It all started with an innocent conversation.

"You know, honey, we have been so busy we really haven't had an opportunity to talk," said Opal.

"Sweetheart, unless we have been on separate vacations, that's all we have done is talk," mused Carl.

Opal couldn't help but laugh. "Well, your 'talking' and my 'talking' are two different things."

"I'm not even going to argue that point. So, what do you want to talk about?"

"Have you had any regrets about coming here? Before you answer, let me say, I love you, I love this place, and I love what our family and friends did for us."

Carl hesitated to see if she wanted to say anything else.

"Is that it? Anything else?"

"Well, yes, there is more. Please understand. I am not upset at all. But, I cannot shake this empty feeling in my heart. We haven't talked about it since we came home from our adventure. It seems that we have tried to substitute anything and everything we could think of to fill the hole, but nothing has worked. Is it just me, or have you felt the same thing?"

Carl didn't answer right away. He wanted to choose his words carefully. The last thing he wanted to do was to spoil the trip.

"You're right, we haven't talked about it in a long time. To be perfectly honest with you, Hon, the emptiness still haunts me after all these years. I can't argue with the fact that I've tried everything in the world to push it away. I thought being good friends, good parents, being super attentive grandparents and the success we've enjoyed in life was enough, but I was wrong. Very honestly, I don't know what to do about it."

Silent tears trickled down their cheeks as they both fought them back. Their hearts were empty, and there was nothing else to say. Carl picked up his plate and walked toward the kitchen. Opal stared out at the ocean and thought, "I guess there really isn't anything else to say. Life is full of mysteries that cannot be solved. I'm just going to drop the subject."

Although they could not shake the emptiness, they both decided to push it aside and enjoy the rest of their stay.

✠

It was the day before they were scheduled to leave for home that they decided to take one last early morning walk on the beach. As they walked along a familiar area they noticed a young man walking toward them. At first they didn't think much of it, but as he drew closer there was something strikingly familiar about him. Strangely, their eyes began to tear up, like a flood of emotions was running through them.

He was only a few feet away when he spoke. "Good morning to you both. Isn't it a beautiful day?"

Carl spoke first. "Yes, it is."

Before another word was spoken the young man reached in to an old worn-out burlap bag that was slung around his shoulder and pulled out two pieces of paper, and with a huge grin on his face handed one to each of them. He didn't say another word. He just looked beyond them as if to keep walking.

"Wait a minute, young man, don't leave yet," implored Carl.

The young man stopped dead in his tracks and said, "Did you want to ask me something?"

"Well, yes I do, if you don't mind. You see, many years ago my wife and I were on this same beach and a young man who looked a lot like you walked up to us and handed us two pieces of paper. He even had the same kind of old burlap bag slung over his shoulder. Please don't think I'm crazy, but this seems so weird. You bear a striking resemblance to that young man."

"Oh, you must be talking about my grandfather. He started a tradition over 50 years ago of walking along the beach and handing out these pieces of paper. I am just carrying on the tradition. As far as the old burlap bag, well, that's a tradition, too. And, if you're wondering, it is the same one!"

He continued, "You would be surprised how many people have said the same thing you just said. I would love to stand here and chat with you longer, but I see there are more people walking on the beach. I need to go."

"Well, at least that clears up the mystery." Before Carl could say another word, the young man said, "I pray both of you have a blessed day." With that he was gone.

As they watched the young man fade into the distance, Opal finally broke the silence.

"Do you feel as strange as I do?" asked Carl. "I'm almost afraid to open the note."

"I feel the same way," replied Opal.

They walked a little further down the beach trying to overcome their mutual fear. Finally, Carl opened his first and it read —"The kingdom of heaven is like unto a merchant man, seeking goodly pearls: Who when he had found one pearl of great price, went and sold all that he had, and bought it."

Carl simply said to Opal, "You can open yours if you want to, but I guarantee you, it says the same thing."

Of course, when he said that she had to open it so they could compare, Opal agreed, "You're right, it does have the same message as yours. So, now what do we do?"

"I have no idea! I guarantee you one thing we're not going to do. We're not about to go on another round the world trip looking for something that we don't even know exists!" They nervously chuckled at each other as they turned to go.

For the next hour or so, they walked in silence along the beach. The feeling of emptiness in their hearts had come back as strong as it was 50 years before when they received the note for the first time.

Carl and Opal walked into the courtyard of the resort and they noticed that several of the local vendors

had set up displays of shops in the area. There was everything from golf, horseback riding, jewelry stores and
gift shops. Walking along several of the displays, Carl
picked up a brochure that looked familiar. It read – G &
F Gift Shop--Trash or Treasure, You Decide."

"Sweetheart, look at this. I'm not sure, but isn't this
the same gift shop that we were going to visit the last
time we were here?"

Opal unfolded the brochure and said, "I believe it
is. I can't believe it's still here after all these years. Why
don't we go for a visit this afternoon? If we don't go
today we won't go at all. Remember, the shuttle leaves
for the airport first thing in the morning."

With undefined excitement, after lunch they made
a beeline down the boardwalk to locate the gift shop.
A lot of new stores had been built, but to their amazement, G & F Gift Shop was still there.

When they walked in the store they felt like they
just stepped out of a time machine. It was the 1960s all
over again. The gift shop itself was small and cluttered
with everything imaginable. Hanging on the walls was
everything from old guitars to rock 'n roll posters from
the 50s and 60s. No doubt the shop was living up to the
sign on the front of the store – "TRASH OR TREAS-
URE – YOU DECIDE"

After browsing around for a few minutes, Carl noticed a large tray of jewelry with a few rings, watches, necklaces, tie clips plus a various assortment of what appeared to be junk jewelry. But half buried under a pile of beads he spotted the top of a bright shimmering pearl. His heart began to race as he tried calmly to ask the young man behind the counter if he could have a closer look into that tray.

As the tray was placed in front of Carl, he tried desperately not to let his eyes focus on the top of that pearl. Somehow, someway, he thought in the back of his mind, "This could be it... what we've been looking for: *The Pearl.*"

Opal became enthralled with an old photo album from the early 1900s. Carl casually got her attention and beckoned her to join him. She could see the excitement in his eyes from across the room as she moved towards him.

The clerk had moved away to help another customer but was very close. Carefully, Carl pointed the top of the pearl out to Opal. That same feeling washed over her. This could be the one. By this time the young man was back in front of Carl and politely said, "Anything that interests you, sir?"

Not wanting to express his excitement, Carl simply replied, "Well, as a man who owned jewelry stores for 40 years, I don't think there's much of real value here."

With a smile on his face the young man simply said, "If you keep looking, you may find something."

Up to this point, Carl had not even touched the pearl, but there was something about it. It was like a magnet, drawing him. He had to see more but didn't want to drive the price up by acting too interested. Carl began to move jewelry around in the tray, always avoiding the pearl but trying to dislodge it from where it was cradled. He had to get a better look!

Carefully, he was able to roll it around to see it from every vantage point, and it was increasingly breathtaking. A quick glance at Opal and he knew that her heart was as stirred as his. THIS IS IT! THIS IS THE ONE! Just seeing it without even owning it yet began to fill their hearts with hope. Carl was so fearful that the young man sensed his excitement that he tried to throw him off by asking the price of almost everything in the tray...but the pearl.

Trying to look very disinterested, Carl acted like he was going to walk away. Suddenly, he turned around and asked to the young man, "Oh, by the way, what are you asking for *the Pearl*?"

Acting very coy, the young man said, "You mean the pearl in the tray you've been looking at for an hour?"

"That's the one," replied Carl.

"I'll have to get my grandfather from the back, because he's the only one that knows the real value of that particular *Pearl*." With that, Carl suspected there was something more here than meets the eye.

The old man walked from the back of the store and stood behind the counter. He was one of those elderly men who just looked like wisdom walking.

"So, you're interested in *The Pearl*?" The way he said *The Pearl* brought chill bumps on Carl and Opal's arms. Carefully, he lifted the pearl from its setting and laid it on a plain white cloth. Carl knew that to heighten the beauty of most any piece of jewelry you would place it on a black velvet piece of cloth. But this pearl did not need to have its beauty heightened. It made everything around it look dull and drab by comparison.

"Is this what you've been looking for?" the elderly man asked. Without worrying any further about his enthusiasm being exposed, Carl and Opal in unison replied, "YES, YES, THIS IS DEFINITELY IT!!"

The old man never blinked an eye. "I'm glad you're that excited, because it's going to take more than mild interest to purchase this pearl. This pearl is the most perfect *Pearl* that exists. It's precious beyond description! It's priceless beyond currency! It's permanently without rival!"

The old man just smiled and said, "In other words, because this pearl is priceless, it will cost you everything."

Quickly, Carl began to mentally calculate all he and Opal had with them and replied to the elderly man, "Everything?"

The old man furrowed his brow and looked straight into his eyes and said, "Everything you have."

Carl's eyes darted from the old man to *The Pearl*, and he thought, "We have to have it, no matter what it costs."

He again leaned over and whispered to Opal, "Hon, we have about $6,000 in cash and about $15,000 in traveler's checks. Let's just give it all without argument." Opal agreed.

Quickly, they laid the cash and cashiers checks on the counter as they begin to sign them one by one. Carl said, "This is a total of $21,000, and I promise that's all we have with us."

The old man held up *The Pearl* and said, "Sir, I don't think you understand. I said everything you have."

"But," Carl said, "that IS everything we have with us."

The old man quickly replied, "It may be all you have with you, but it's certainly not all you have."

"Of course we have more than is with us, but certainly you don't mean everything we have everywhere?" Carl asked.

The old man took out a piece of paper and slid it across the counter to Carl. "That's exactly what I mean. If you want this pearl it will cost you and your wife everything."

Somehow in their hearts Carl and Opal knew it was worth it. To anyone who had never really seen this *Pearl* it was foolishness, but to those whose eyes had beheld *The Pearl*, it was well worth everything.

With that, Carl began to list all of their assets from bank accounts to property, from 401K's to jewelry acquired, from cars to boats and from other investments to other hard assets... everything.

"Is this everything?" asked the old man, as he studied the paper.

"Yes, that's it, everything."

Gently the elderly man asked, "Do you have children and grandchildren?"

Before he could answer, Opal pulled him aside. "My love, do you realize what he is asking us to do?"

Carl didn't hesitate. "I don't fully, and I can't explain it, but I believe with all my heart it's worth it. Please, let's believe."

With that, Carl turned back to the old man and said, "Yes, we do. Do you want us to write their names down as well?"

"Yes, everyone's name and age, please."

With a shaky hand, Carl began to list the names and ages of their children and grandchildren. He showed the list to Opal to make sure he didn't leave anyone out. Opal put her hand on his shoulder and said, "I don't know how to explain what I'm feeling right now, but I do believe it's worth it." His look said, "I agree."

Again Carl slid the paper over to the old man. While he waited for him to read the list, Carl said, "That's it, that's everything, all we possess materially and everyone we count precious in life."

The old man looked up and said, "Are you sure this is everything?"

"Yes, I am sure. My wife and I went over the list twice. I know we didn't leave anyone off!"

Pointing to Opal he said, "I don't see her name on the list. And, I don't see your name on the list. I said, everything!" He slid the paper back across the counter.

All of a sudden, like a title wave of truth, it hit them. *This Pearl* is really requiring all we are and all we have.... Not only our dreams for the rest of our life but our hopes for the future in our children and grandchildren: EVERYTHING!

With one last look at each other to confirm their feelings, they each printed and signed their names at the bottom of the paper and slid it back to the elderly man.

By this time, Carl and Opal were overwhelmed with emotion. On one hand they mysteriously knew something was changing and this was the best choice of their life. On the other hand, flashes of doubt and fear began to run through their minds. "How would this all play out? What do we do now? How do we explain this to our children and grandchildren? What will our future look like?" But, for all the fleeting doubts, they were both overwhelmed with a sense of peace, joy and assurance they had never known.

The old man surveyed the list a third time and tenderly said, "Well done, the transaction is over. It is finished. *The Pearl* is yours!"

With that, he took *The Pearl*, wrapped it in a cloth, placed it in a box, and handed it to Carl. As Carl reached out to take the box, his heart was about to explode. He put his arm around Opal and started to leave holding *The Perfect Pearl* in his hand.

"Hold on a minute. Don't leave yet," said the old man, "There's one more thing."

"Sir, there is nothing left to give. We've left it all behind with you," Carl said respectfully.

With a large, warm smile that almost glowed, the storeowner held up the paper and asked them to come back to the counter. Carefully, he folded the paper, handed it to them and said, "Here, I want you to take this. You see, I don't have need of any of these things you've written down, not even the cash and cashiers checks. I want you to take them home with you and cherish the blessings of your family and all you've worked so hard to accumulate in life. I give them all back for you to steward and enjoy all the days of your life."

Carl and Opal stood there speechless as he continued, "But, if one day I show up and have need of any of those assets.., from a car to a home from bank account to investments, I want you to remember to whom they really belong. And, one cold winter evening, while sitting around a warm fire with your family, I may come knocking at your door. And if I do, remember to whom your family really belongs; even your precious grandchildren.

And finally, Carl, when the season is over on earth for your darling bride, as difficult as it may be for you, I want you to release her to me. Whether it's property, money or family, remember, you have given it all over to my care. Carl and Opal, I make you a promise: that all of my intentions towards you and those you love will always be to bless you, even when you don't understand. I'm not asking you to understand, I'm only asking that you trust me."

This time they were not only speechless but numbed, but accepting of his words. Looking deeply into his eyes as if searching for something, they thanked him, gave him a hug and left the shop. They had found their treasure at G & F Gift Shop among a lot of trash.

Walking on the beach back to the villa, Pearl in hand, they both felt something strange happening in their heart. With each step, with each heartbeat, something was changing. The sun seemed brighter, the sky was bluer, even the air smelled cleaner. If there were any other people on the beach, they didn't notice. They didn't have to talk, because they both knew something had changed.

When they got back to their room Carl said, "Let's open the box. I want to look at *The Pearl* again."

Carl handed the box to Opal and said, "You open it, Hon, my hands are shaking too badly."

Opal walked over to the kitchen counter and opened the box.

She gasped, "The box is empty!"

Carl walked over to the counter and said, "Not funny, Sweetheart, let me see it."

To Carl's amazement and shock, the box was indeed empty. They didn't know whether to laugh or cry, but after a few moments of stunned silence, they burst into laughter.

Carl said, "I don't care! Somehow, I believe that we have something on the inside of us that's more priceless than the pearl missing from the box!"

Opal agreed. "Honey, I don't pretend to understand all that just happened, but one thing I know, something is different on the inside, and that's what really matters. All those years, all that searching... now the void and emptiness are gone for good. I can't wait to go home and tell our children what we have found."

After a few more minutes of discussion, Carl looked at Opal and asked, "What time is it?"

"5:30 pm."

"I don't think it's too late. The store is probably still open. Grab the box. I'm not leaving until the old man explains what just happened to us."

Carl and Opal had discovered a destiny moment: the moment when eternity interrupts time and everything is turned 'right side up'. The moment when you cry from the depths of your being, "It is well, it is well with my soul." The moment of experiencing things you can't possibly explain. It begins with knowing that you know, that you know, that you know something beyond words.

There are two great events in a man's life – one when he is born, and the other when he finds out why! They already knew the 'when' – now they were going back to G & F to find out the 'why'.

# CHAPTER TEN

# An Exciting Transformation

Carl stood at the bottom of the stairs of their home waiting to greet the children. Looking at his watch, he surprised himself with his unanticipated patience. They had invited the children over for the evening to share about their trip and discovery, and he wanted to make certain that he and Opal were both at the front door when they arrived.

Normally, he would have been very impatient with Opal being a little slow, but since they returned from Jamaica strange feelings like patience were his companions. He felt a different kind of love than he'd known before: a peace that seemed to pass all understanding and a deep joy that was unspeakable. Opal was experiencing the same emotions, and their entire existence seemed to revolve around those changes that *The Pearl* had brought.

"Just give me ten more minutes, and I'll be down. I think everything is ready in the kitchen. All I have to do is warm up the bread," called Opal from the upstairs bedroom.

Carl and Opal had been home for only two days, but they couldn't wait to have a family gathering and share with everyone the exciting news.

It had been obvious to everyone who greeted them at the airport, upon their return from the second honeymoon, that something had happened. On the previous arrival, the atmosphere was dark and gloomy. This time everything was different. The glow on their faces announced to everyone that something momentous had happened; something life-changing. They could not attribute the change to the joy and excitement of a second honeymoon. No, there had to be more.

The children and grandchildren finally arrived, and Opal made it downstairs in time. Even though they had seen each other at the airport two days prior those two days seemed like an eternity. They really didn't want to eat, but out of great respect for their parents they all restrained themselves from asking questions.

Finally, the meal was finished, and it was time to hear about the trip. It was a tradition for everyone to sit around in a big circle with the grandkids sitting on the floor. Tonight would be no different.

Carl raised his hand to get everyone's attention.

"Kids, Mom and I have something we want to share with you. I know you want to hear about the trip, and we can certainly talk about all the fun things we did later. But first and foremost, we want you to know – WE FOUND WHAT WE HAVE BEEN LOOKING FOR! WE FOUND THE PERFECT, PRICELESS PEARL, AND WE ARE FOREVER CHANGED."

Opal burst out laughing and said, "Please forgive my excitement. I guess you can tell that Dad and I are very happy – no, not happy, joyful would be a better word. Maybe both, anyway, I think you understand what I'm trying to say. Since we have found the meaning of T*he Pearl of Great Price*, we have been on cloud nine. That void, that emptiness that nothing seemed adequate to fill, is gone."

By now the atmosphere in the room was electric. Everyone tried to talk at once. Finally, the oldest daughter asked everyone to hush for a minute and let her speak.

"Mom and Dad, I think I speak for everyone when I say it's obvious something has happened to you. I also think everyone is wondering how a pearl could change you so much. I'm not trying to be skeptical, but you went almost around the world looking for this so-called *Perfect Pearl* and didn't find it. Now, you're telling us that you went on a 10 day trip to Jamaica and found it?"

Carl let her finish. Finally he said, "I know you must be confused. The best thing for us to do is to start at the beginning of our discovery and explain to you how we found *The Perfect Pearl*.

For the next hour or so Opal told them everything that had happened from the time they arrived in Jamaica. She started with the strange encounter with the young Jamaican on the beach. She told them that he was the grandson of the man they met over 50 years ago at the same spot. And, that he gave them the same message on the same kind of paper from the same old worn burlap bag.

They skipped over a few of the details, because they wanted to move quickly to what happened at the gift shop.

Opal said to Carl, "You tell the rest, Honey. I'm just going to sit here and be still, because my heart is so full that I can't talk." They all laughed knowing their mom.

Carl continued, "Now comes the good stuff."

He told them about finding G & F Gift Shop. He then told them about the old man and *The Pearl*.

"You know, we looked around for a few minutes and I saw this tray of watches and assorted jewelry sitting in the display window. Right in the middle was a pearl. When the old man's assistant brought over the tray I noticed immediately that this was no ordinary pearl. I knew then and there I had to have it. When I asked for a price the young man said that I would have to talk to his grandfather. Little did I know the conversation with the old man would change us forever!"

Carl continued to explain how cool and nonchalant he tried to be when he negotiated for *The Pearl*.

"The old man told me *The Pearl* was priceless. But, that didn't stop me. I made him an offer, and he promptly told me it would cost me everything."

Carl went on to explain what happened when the old man told him what it would cost. When Carl came to the part of listing all of their valuables, he tried his best to explain why the old man kept sliding the piece of paper back across the counter. The man said he wanted everything, including every family member on the list!

"Each time he asked me if there was anything else to add to the list, I told him no – and each time he challenged me. I realized there was always something else to add. Finally, he was convinced we had given up our rights to everything and gave us *The Pearl*."

Their youngest granddaughter, Kadie Jewel, spoke up and said, "Pawpaw, you were willing to give up your rights to all of us?"

Seeing tears in her eyes he quickly said, "Sweetheart, let me explain. It's not what you think."

Then Carl explained to them that after making the exchange they were about to walk out the door when the old man told them to come back.

"He then handed us the list and said he didn't need anything we listed. He just wanted us to know that he was now the rightful owner of everything. He explained that we are just caretakers and stewards over everything that was written on the paper. It all belonged to him. He could call for it any time he wanted, and we had no right to complain or be bitter about any of it!"

Their oldest son spoke up and said, "Dad, I don't understand. Maybe, if you show us *The Pearl*, we will see what you saw."

Carl simply smiled and said, "Let me finish, and I think everything will be made clear."

He told them about leaving the gift shop and rushing back to the room and how they opened the box to look at *The Pearl* and it was gone!

There was a collective gasp in the room.

Carl continued, "We hurried back to the gift shop to find the old man. Sure enough, he was sitting there almost as if he were waiting on us to come back. I put the box on the counter and said it was empty, but for some reason we were not upset. We just wanted him tell us what's going on."

The old man walked around from behind the counter and put his arms around both of us.

"At that moment he taught us the most valuable truth we had ever learned. It has changed us forever. The truth he gave us is the same truth I want to give to you."

"I won't be able to quote word for word what the old man said, but I will do my best to give you the essence of his teaching. He started by explaining the meaning of the note that was handed to us on the beach so many years before."

At this point, Carl pulled out the old wrinkled paper they were handed 50 years ago. Yes, he had saved it!

Then he said, "The Scripture in the note is from a parable Jesus told in Matthew 13 verses 45 & 46. It reads, "Again, the Kingdom of Heaven is like unto a merchant man, seeking goodly pearls: Who, when he had found one pearl of great price, went and sold all that he had, and bought it."

"The wise elderly man went on to explain that the merchant in the story is anyone who is in search of the true meaning of why we are here on planet earth. He said, 'The reason you could not find *The Pearl of Great Price* is that you thought it was something you could buy or earn or even something you deserved. You traveled around the world searching for the elusive Pearl and came up empty time and time again. Your hearts remained empty, because you thought the pearl was something, when in fact, it is SOMEONE, and that SOMEONE is Jesus Christ the only begotten Son of God.'

He continued, 'You must understand that without Christ you will always be empty and lost. The emptiness you have felt for all of these years is not just not knowing why you were put on planet earth, but not knowing Christ. You thought being a good husband, a great father, and grandfather was enough, but it wasn't. Hard work and loyalty are to be admired, but that was not enough. Nothing in this life could ever fill the void deep inside, but that void, that emptiness is for a reason.'

'You see,' he said to us, 'men will never seek after Jesus, but rather, Jesus is seeking after men. It's true there are many seekers today who are more often than not seeking help, social contact, or financial gain. The goodly pearls in the story are one man seeking wealth, the other seeking fame, another education and yet another to be honored.  All of these are nothing more than counterfeit pearls. But seldom are they seeking real truth. This is not to say that mankind isn't looking for something real, but they aren't looking in the right direction. That's why Jesus put that hunger in your hearts over 50 years ago and set you on this journey to seek so you would find HIM, Jesus Christ is *The Pearl of Great Price.*'

At this point the old man opened an old tattered Bible and read these verses to us:

Romans 3: 11 – "There is no one who understands; there is no one who seeks God."

Romans 3:23-"For all have sinned, and come short of the glory of God."

Romans 6:23-"For the wages of sin is death: but the gift of God is eternal life through Jesus Christ our Lord."

Romans 5:8-"But God showed His love toward us, in that while we were yet sinners, Christ died for us."

Romans 10:9,10-"That if thou shalt confess with thy mouth the Lord Jesus, and shall believe in thine heart that God has raised him from the dead, thou shall be saved."

The old man began to weep and told us that Jesus died on Calvary's cross over 2,000 years ago and shed His blood for our sins. Jesus died for us and because of us. All other religious leaders of the world only want you to follow them and their teachings. But the issue in Christianity is that you CAN NOT follow Christ until the sin issue is dealt with first. The Bible says, "without the shedding of blood there is no forgiveness of sin." Christ shed His precious blood for you and me. Forgiveness of sin is what keeps us from the Kingdom of God and the King of that Kingdom is Jesus, our *Pearl of Great Price*."

Carl stopped talking for a moment and looked around the room. He wanted to see their reaction to what he was saying. The family was mesmerized by their father's words.

So, he continued, "The old man stood up and walked behind the counter. I thought maybe he was finished. I was wrong. He reached under the counter and brought out another pearl.

The old man held it up for us to look at and continued talking."

'You see this pearl? Crush it and all you will have is lime or ordinary chalk. The value of the pearl is how it comes into existence. You cannot carve one or cut one like a ruby or a diamond. If you cut a pearl you might as well throw it away, because it becomes worthless.

I'm sure you learned many things about pearls on your adventure. But, let me remind you, a pearl is created in the heart of a living oyster; in the deepest, darkest part of the ocean. It begins as a grain of sand introduced inside the shell. It cuts and digs into the tender inner tissues of the oyster. The oyster's response is to secrete a substance called Nacre, also known as Mother of Pearl. Layer upon layer is formed around that grain of sand until it becomes a beautiful pearl!

A beautiful pearl is nothing more than the oyster's answer to what wounded it. A pearl would never come into existence if the oyster was unwilling to cover that which had cut it.

Then he asked me, 'Carl, do you and Opal understand that is a beautiful picture of salvation in Christ? Our part was the cutting, and God's part was the covering! Man's sin was an intrusion that cut the heart of God. And, like that grain of sand, we were trapped, held captive with no way of escape on our own. But while ours was the cutting, God's was the covering.'

Thank God that Calvary covers it all! The cross was God's answer to man's sin! The innocent died for the guilty—both in the garden of Eden with sheepskins to cover man's body and on the cross of Calvary to cover man's sin.'

I then asked the old man, 'If salvation is free, then why did we have to list all of our valuable possessions?' His reply was brief but profound.'

'Good question, Carl. Let me see if I can explain.'

'Salvation is indeed free – but not cheap. It cost God His very best to provide salvation and freedom from sin's deadly grasp. He had to bankrupt heaven in order to redeem us back to himself. His son willingly left Heaven's home, born of a virgin, lived a sinless life, died on the cross in our place, was raised from the dead on the third day to be Lord of the living and the dead. The writing down of all of your assets, including your family, was my way of emphasizing salvation is about exchange. The Bible is very clear... when you give your life to Christ... you are giving him EVERYTHING! JESUS BECOMES LORD OF ALL, BECAUSE HE GAVE HIS ALL FOR YOU. This will seem very unclear in the beginning of your faith walk. But the longer you live for Christ the greater will be your understanding and willingness to lose all, to gain Him.'

"The old man scribbled some things on a piece of paper, and said to always keep this with us. I still have it with me. Let me read it to you."

Carl unfolded the piece of paper and read to the group:

*He will exchange His righteousness for your sin.*
*He will exchange His riches for your poverty.*
*He will exchange His wholeness for your brokenness.*
*He will exchange His joy for your sadness.*
*He will exchange His fullness for your emptiness.*
*He will exchange His peace for your turmoil.*
*He will exchange His life for yours.*

"The old man told us that there would come a time when we would need to be reminded of all God did for us.

He didn't stop there, but continued to talk to us.

'To some, salvation is just an escape from eternal judgment, for others they think it is a cheap ticket to heaven. But, that's a great misunderstanding of biblical salvation. God gave His very best and expects our faithfulness to Jesus in return. He will never be satisfied when we give Him the scraps and the leftovers of our life.'

He read another verse from the Bible: I Corinthians 6:20- 'For you were bought with a price: therefore glorify and honor God in your body, and in your spirit, which are God's.'

Just then, the old man tenderly reached down and took our hands and said, 'I think it would be a good time for us to stop and pray.'"

He prayed the most beautiful prayer we had ever heard. All I know is, when he finished his prayer, your mother and I gave EVERYTHING, and I mean EVERYTHING, to Jesus. From that moment to this moment, our lives have been transformed.

As we began to leave the store, the elderly man embraced us and said, 'Welcome, brother and sister, to the Family of God. This is the most important decision of your life with eternity at the other end. I cannot promise you it will always be easy, but it will be learning, growing and changing more than you ever dreamed possible.'

We started to leave, but I had one more question I couldn't get out of my mind, so I asked the owner. 'Would you mind telling me what the G & F stands for on the sign for your shop?' Our friend replied, 'I thought you would have figured that out by now. Why, it stands for GRACE AND FAITH, because it's by grace through faith that you have found your Precious Pearl.'"

The atmosphere in the living room was filled with holy silence when Carl spoke.

"I know your mother and I have given you a lot to take in. But, I want you to know we are changed from the inside out! We thought we had to travel to foreign lands and spend thousands of dollars to find what was already ours for the asking. We were wrong – HOWEVER, WE REALLY DIDN'T FIND *THE PEARL OF GREAT PRICE*, HE FOUND US. And, we believe He has made His way into this living room through us tonight. We could have no greater desire in life, for all of you, than to know that all of our children and grandchildren walk in truth. Our desire is for you to know the love of God and the peace and joy we have in knowing Jesus our risen Lord."

After a few minutes of quiet, this time their middle granddaughter, Marlee Kaye, stood up and said, "I may never understand everything you just said, but I want… no, I must have what you have!" She was Pawpaw's favorite, because she captured his heart in a beautiful, polka dot dress when she was very young.

One by one they all stood and said the same thing. Holding hands they made a giant circle, and Carl led them all in prayer to the cross of Christ. Salvation truly came to the entire household that evening.

There was lots of laughter, and no shortage of tears that night as the family circle was completed. What started years before with a simple note had now come full circle to include an entire family! And they knew deep in their hearts that the circle would be unbroken through all eternity.

Lying in bed hours later with hearts bursting with faith and peace, Carl turned to Opal in tears, "Eighteen inches is really all we had to travel."

"What are you talking about,?" asked Opal.

"I simply mean, you don't have to travel thousands of miles to find *The Pearl of Great Price*. It is a short trip – normally about 18 inches – from your head to your heart!"

As they gazed at one another in the soft light of the bedside lamp, they felt more in love than ever. Their wrinkled faces testified that they were in their last season on planet earth. But now there was no fear of the end. Their newly found love for Jesus had also given them a deeper love for each other. Their love for each other had carried them through many storms; one day God's love for them would carry them through the final storm and bring them safely home.

As Carl and Opal went off to sleep that glorious night, there was joy in their life and a knowledge in their hearts that they would "Dwell in the House of The Lord Forever."

### THE BEGINNING

Dear Reader, let me share a parting illustration and final observations.

# Illustration

Barbara Krensavage insisted that clams were not a regular part of her diet. Yet, one snowy evening in December, she found herself craving an old recipe, so she brought home four dozen quahogs-a clam particularly abundant between Cape Cod and New Jersey. Mr. Krensavage was in the mist of shucking the shellfish for dinner when he discovered one that looked like it was dead. It had a different color to it and he thought it was diseased. As he was about to discard it, Mrs. Krensavage took a closer look.

It wasn't dead. In fact, inside the live clam was a rare and possibly priceless, purple pearl. Experts estimate that roughly one in two million quahog clams contains a gem-quality pearl like the one found by the Krensavages. Due to the great rarity of the find it has been difficult to even place a value on it, though some have estimated the pearl to be worth hundreds of thousands of dollars.

# Observations

The message Christ brought to the world was one that spoke openly of a Kingdom among us, where, like this discovery of the Krensavages, all is not as it may first appear. In a world that seems more marked by disease than promise there is, hidden in this life, a treasure worth selling all we have to possess as our own. Where there seems to be a world of stagnant hope and deteriorating vision, there is promise of living water and signs of its presence. Although the world around us is marked by the power of death, there is life among us that is stronger than death itself. Now we see through a glass darkly, but for those who will see, the kingdom Christ will show us He is here, and He is real: *The Pearl of Great Price.*

We who are in Christ must be willing to part with all for Him; to leave all to follow Him. If we are to love and serve Him, we must cheerfully leave behind all that stands in opposition to or competition with Christ, even though dear to us. Our one cry must be, "Not my will, but Thy will be done."

Anything that stands as a roadblock to His will threatens to be the greatest stumbling block to our life. A man may buy gold cheaply, but not his *Pearl of Great Price.* Whatever the cost, the demand, or sacrifice, it will be worth it all when we see Jesus.

# Epilogue

This short story began as a labor of love for me. I sat at my computer and typed, with my mind racing one hundred miles an hour. I think the romantic in me became more evident to me the longer I wrote. My desire is for the story to display genuine warmth with a sense of real life scenarios. I want you to be able to sit back, for a quiet evening by a warm fire, and be transported to the feet of Jesus. At the same time, I want you to reflect on what's ultimately the most important part of life.

Therefore, I want to share a few things from the story that may be hidden to you.

Carl and Opal are the names of Billie Kaye's (my wife) parents. Even though they have both passed from this life, I wanted to honor their memory. After all, outside salvation, they gave me the greatest gift I've ever received.

The three granddaughters (each my favorite) are actually the names of three of my granddaughters.

Meagan Ashley (Rush), my oldest granddaughter, is the daughter of Mark and Gretchen (my daughter) Rush.

Kadie Jewel (Tsika), my youngest granddaughter, is the daughter of Thom (my son) and Kelley Tsika.

Marlee Kaye (Tsika), my middle granddaughter, is the daughter of Paul (my son) and Melanie Tsika.

The three children are the names of our children.

Gretchen, our oldest, is Gretchen Tsika Rush. She and her husband, Mark, have three wonderful girls of their own: Meagan, Marissa and Malory.

Paul, who is Paul II, our oldest son, is married to Melanie, and they have four children: Emily (with her son Jaylen), Demetri, Marlee and Zeke.

Thom, who is our youngest son, is married to Kelley, and they have three children: Shelby, Jake and Kadie Jewel.

The setting in Ocho Rios is in Jamaica. Billie and I have vacationed there and love the people of Jamaica. We've had some wonderful times ministering in Jamaica and have many dear friends who live there.

The 50th Anniversary date (April 28) is actually our anniversary date. And in 2016, Billie Kaye and I will celebrate our 50th Wedding Anniversary, if we're still here on planet earth: Fifty wonderful years, for me, with the woman I love from here to eternity and back.

As far as always flying First Class, well, I'll leave that up to you to decide. One thing for certain, it best describes the wonderfully blessed life the Lord has given us with our family, friends and ministry since *The Pearl* found us.

# Introducing the cast in order
## of their appearance

*Carl and Opal* represent every man and woman born of Adam's race who is searching for the meaning of life and its fulfillment.

*The Void* is that thirst in every person's life that can't be quenched with the things of this world. Jesus said, "if you drink of the wells of this world you will thirst again and again.

*The tall lanky Jamaican* on the beaches of Ocho Rios represents the blessed Holy Spirit who confronts mankind with the gospel, draws them to Christ, and indwells those who believe.

*The parchment* given to Carl and Opal on the beach is their first introduction to the gospel that exposes their emptiness but also hints of God's promise.

Traveling the world looking for *The Pearl* represents man's desperate search for life's meaning in a vain pursuit of empty promises.

Carl and Opal, *giving up on their dream*, is the story of all mankind's midnight, desperately searching for peace, before the dawn breaks.

The *G&F* (trash or trinket-you decide) gift shop is the Grace through Faith by which we are saved. Ephesians 2:8 "For by grace ye are saved through faith, it's a gift of God not of works lest any man should boast."

*The Elderly Shop Owner* represents God The Father who reveals the high cost of owning *Your Pearl*: that precious *Pearl* that He sent; *The Pearl* who willingly came, only to be crushed under the weight of man's sin. After only three days The Father raised His precious *Pearl* up from death's dark grave to be Lord of the living and the dead. As people who search for *The Pearl*, we come to a desperate willingness to pay any price once we've seen *The Pearl* for ourselves, Jesus Christ the Lord.

# More Resources by Paul E. Tsika

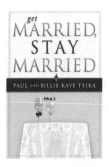

Book, Audio Book/CD/DVD,
Workbook

Book, Audio CD

Book, Audio Book

Book

Book, Audio Book

Book

**Plow-On Publications**
P.E.T. Ministries, Inc. | Restoration Ranch
www.plowon.org  |  361-588-7190